The Wrong Man

A Novel of the American Civil War

by

Michal Howden

"Nobody but McClellan would not have attacked."

Confederate General Joseph Johnston

"McClellan is to me one of the mysteries of the war."

Union General US Grant

for my family

all my family

with a special light on my wonderful wife

without whom not one word would have been written - MH

Thanks and a note of appreciation...

I would like to express my sincere thanks to Mr. John Scannell and Ms. Dawn Haas Knight, authors and superb English teachers. Sincere thanks also go to another superb teacher and lover of the Oxford Comma, Ms. Jayne Shubat. Thanks for the outstanding editing and support. Above and beyond, Jayne. Thank you. A thank you as well to Mr. Topher Howden. Cannot thank you enough for the design work and the last push across the finish line.

Without y'all, the book does not exist. And Dawn, Jayne and Tophs? Go Hoosiers.

Cover art created by Ms. Carol Richard

Covers designed by Mr. Topher Howden

Cover photography by Michal Howden

Chapter 1

"Well, well, what do we have here, Sergeant? A Rebel spy headed for the gallows?"

The questioner, a tall, ruddy, weather-worn man, rode up to the buckboard and pulled up on the reins. He gazed at the wagon, pulling a kerchief from his pocket. He mopped his brow, wiping away grime, sweat, dust and dirt. Washington D. C. was both hot and humid in August and the roads were always a mess, no matter what the season. Dusty with the heat, muddy with rain, icy with the cold. Take your pick.

The rider leaned closer to the buckboard. "Obviously, a dangerous, traitorous Rebel spy!" he declared.

The rider, Thomas Henderson, was looking at two forlorn figures who sat side by side on the top bench of the buckboard wagon. One figure was slight, a boy, a child? His small frame was draped under a much too large blue Union private's overcoat. His face was filthy. His hair was a tangled, dirty heap. Though Thomas wasn't close enough to swear it was true, he was sure the boy smelled. The boy did not appear to be happy.

Next to the small figure sat a grizzled sergeant, Sergeant Emerson of the US Second Rhode Island. He did not appear to be happy either. The horseman knew the good sergeant. A few weeks ago, they had traveled down the road to Manassas together. Thomas had no idea who the boy was, and he was curious. He leaned a bit closer.

"Whew! I'm not sure how dangerous a spy he is, Sergeant, or how old he is, but he sure is filthy! Do you have to clean him up before you hang him?" the horseman asked curiously.

The boy wrenched toward the horseman. "Damn no, I ain't no Rebel spy!" he quickly spat out. "I'm Union true, through and through and . . ."

Before another word left his mouth, the sergeant gave a quick, almost effortless tug on the rope that circled the boy's waist. The boy instantly jerked back toward the burly man. As he snapped back, the sergeant's large hand snaked out and smacked the boy half heartedly on the head.

"Mind your dirty mouth, boy," the sergeant mumbled the command over a large, moist plug of chewing tobacco. Holding up one finger toward the horseman, he leaned over and spat. He coughed and maneuvered the wad around in his mouth.

"Ahem, sorry 'bout his language, Thomas. He's spent too much time hanging around soldiers, I reckon. Picked hisself up a big ole slew of bad habits." He leaned sideways and spat again over the wagon's side. "No, nothing as easy or simple as a spy," he continued, "just a young dirty, smelly, disagreeable, obnoxious brat!" Sergeant Emerson glared at the boy. "A brat the colonel done stuck me with babysittin'!"

Thomas laughed. "And just what did you do that was so bad, Sergeant Emerson, that the colonel gave this young, dirty brat to you?"

Sergeant Emerson slowly looked heavenward, conveying to all the world that he could not, for the life of him, think of one tiny reason he was being punished with this assignment. "Well, there might have been this one late night poker game . . ." His voice trailed off, and he continued to look at the far horizon.

The horseman laughed heartily. "I've been in a few of those games with you! Now I understand!" He leaned down and extended a long arm toward the roped boy. "Thomas Henderson, of New York," he said. "Nice to meet you. And you are?"

The boy glared, fearing he was being made fun of. He was dad-gummed not going to be the butt of some stranger's joke. Then the man's words sunk in. Had this man just said he was from New York?

"Are you from her?" the boy squeaked. "Are you from Aunt Hezbayla?" He leaned as far away from the man as he could.

"Aunt Hezababayla?" came Thomas's confused answer. "Well, no, I don't believe I've had the pleasure . . ." Henderson clearly did not understand the question. He sat with his empty hand extended, a puzzled look on his face.

Not about to be taken in, the boy decided it was a trap. Well, he was too smart to fall for that. He'd learned far too much in these last few months. His attitude instantly changed. An extremely insincere smile appeared as he reached for the stranger's hand. "Thomas Jefferson. Pleased to meet you."

Henderson guffawed. "Thomas Jefferson! Why, you look remarkably well preserved for a man who's been dead thirty some years." Henderson shook the boy's hand as he laughed.

"Now you see what I have to deal with?" asked the exasperated sergeant. "Thomas Jefferson, indeed. Why this un' would sooner lie than take a breath. Sooner lie than eat his dinner! Sooner lie that get his pay, not that he's getting any of that anymore." He paused and glared at the boy. "If he did collect any pay at anytime!" He sent another blow. "The truth is scarcer than hen's teeth around this one," he lamented.

This time, the blow missed. The boy saw it coming and recoiled just in time.

"This here," Sergeant Emerson continued, "is Jake Bunten. Least ways that's what he claimed one time. We don't really know where he's from. We've heard a couple of stories on that." He paused, remembering. "We heard at least a couple of different versions."

"Bunten! Well I bet your school mates must have called you Butts," Thomas said.

Jake instantly bunched his fists, his face flushing. "Not more than once, they wouldn't have," he said, lifting his small fists toward Henderson. "And that's not my name!"

Henderson threw his hands up in mock surrender as he laughed. "Well, clearly not," he said. "As I can certainly see! I was thinking you were a small bird of a boy, but now I think you must be a bantam!"

Jake glared at him. Now he was sure he was being made fun of. "A bantam, what the hell's that?" The sergeant's hand shot out again, but Jake was looking for it and again avoided the blow.

"Why a fighting bird, of course," said Henderson with humor in this voice. "Don't you think it fits?" He leaned a little closer to the boy. "You have had some learning, haven't you, Son?" Without waiting for an answer, Henderson turned back to the sergeant.

"So what's Banty's story, Sergeant?" Henderson asked, "How'd you come to rope him and brand him? And who's Aunt Whomever and how did you come to be his captor?"

"Banty!" Jake indignantly sputtered. "Banty! And I sure never been caught and branded!" He paused to glare hatefully at the sergeant. "Not that I haven't been abused in all sorts of other ways..."

The rope tugged again and this time there was no way to avoid the cupped hand.

Sergeant Emerson glared down at the boy and then returned his attention to Henderson. The expression on his face seemed to say it all - See what I have to deal with?

But the sergeant's look softened as he began his tale. "As near as we can figure he ran off from some place out West to come join the army. He says he enlisted in Washington D.C. and was mustered into the Second Ohio. He said he was at Bull Run but then he lies about everything. He probably stole those clothes he's a'wearing. Probably been stealing food as well."

"Well, well Banty," Henderson said, looking at the boy with a new expression on his face. "That's quite the story. How'd he come to end up with the Second Rhode Island?"

"That part of the story hasn't been made clear. Just turned up here and started acting like he belonged. It didn't take us long to figure out things weren't adding up."

Thomas gave the boy a long, thoughtful look. "Alright Banty, I've heard a bit from the learned Sergeant Emerson, care to give me any more information?"

"No, Sir, I would not," came the quick reply. "A man's business is his own." The boy abruptly crossed his dirty skinny arms across an equally dirty, skinny chest. It was clear he had not been overeating (or over bathing) recently.

Henderson chuckled at the boy's response. "Usually, I would agree with that, but when you sit here trussed and ready for the oven? Some would say that might change a few things. Come now, enlighten me."

Jacob stared stonily ahead, refusing even to give the man a glance.

"Fine, fine, have it your way, Banty. So Sergeant, what's to become of this young one?"

"Well, Sir, after a lot of discussion and debate, the decision was to turn him over to the kind folks at St. Anne's Foundling Home."

"Why, that's here in the capital, isn't it?"

"That's the one, Thomas, right here in Washington D.C."

"But I still don't know how all this came about, Sergeant."

"Well, Sir, it was like this. Once we got back from Manassas, suddenly Jake here is in our camp. Said he got separated from his regiment during the skeedadle. Well, there was enough going on after that fiasco, as you well now, so nobody paid much attention to him. Turns out there were more than a couple of camp-rats around. Course some men brought their families with them, so it was hard to know who was who.

"But that all changed when the Colonel got his bad news. Short time after Bull Run he got the letter that told him his own son had died of the fever. Well that changed it all. He declared that no more children would be dying here and no more children would be living here. He ordered all of the camp-rats wrangeled up and sent out. If they had family, they went there. If they didn't, well other arrangements had to be made. Jake here drew the straw that took him to St. Anne's." Sergeant Emerson paused for a minute, looking at Jake. "That's on account of him never mentioning no kin before. No pa, no ma and certainly no aunt...aunt... aunt whatever he said." He gave Jake a puzzled look, as if trying to figure out what might be the truth. He paused to send another stream of tobacco over the wagon's edge.

"So that's his tale. Yes sir, it is. We're just arranging his transportation this afternoon. They're ready for his arrival. All the details have been worked out. We've even taken up a collection among the boys to contribute. He's all set."

"Course, he shouldn't be there long, he's near apprentice age. We don't of course know his real age, but looks be told, he's close. Yes, Sir, that's his tale."

"My tale" the sergeant continued, "is I got snookered with the job of babysittin' and takin' him on into the city. All because of one simple little poker game…" the sergeant's voice drifted off.

"But what about his family?" Henderson mildly protested, "What about this Aunt he mentioned, Aunt Hepzibah or whatever it was?"

"Today is the first time he's ever mentioned any family name, or any name at all. We've never heard word one about her or anyone else for that matter. Thinking on it, I reckon it's just another one of his lies." Sergenant Emerson said tiredly.

"It is not," Jake suddenly erupted. "Hezbayla! Aunt Hezbayla is her name and she is kin. She's kin and I can prove it!" He pulled a dirty tarred haversack up from the wagon floor. He rummaged in it for a few minutes and then pulled out a tattered envelope. In bold handwriting, the address read "Miss Hezbayla Bunten, Chittenango, NY"

"Chittenango, NY" Sergerant Emerson said in a surprised voice. "Where in tarnation is that?"

"Upstate New York, I believe", Thomas absently said, staring at the envelope.

"Is that your home, boy?"

Suddenly, Jacob's words poured out in a rush. "I was born in Indiana. Ma and Pa are dead. Died of a fever. My only living relation is my Pa's sister, this here,

Hezbayla Bunten. I've never laid eyes on her. She's never laid eyes on me." He stopped, as suddenly as he had started. He stared down at his battered boots. "I was on my way to Chittenango. I was to live with her." He looked up at the men. "I took a small detour."

"So you've run away from home, heh?" The Sergeant declared.

"This woman is expecting you? She's waiting for you?" said Thomas, at almost the same instant.

"I never run away from her! I've never met her!" He said, with a defiant glance at the Sergeant. He turned to Henderson. "She's never known me. Never seen the women in my life!" He repeated, "I've never met the woman." Suddenly his shoulders sagged. He didn't say another word because Jake just realized that in his haste to prove his honesty, he had made a mistake. A big mistake.

Emerson and Henderson looked at each other silently for a moment.

"Well" Sergerant Emerson sadly said "I reckon that cat is out of that bag now. We wuz all set to hand off the urchin and be done with him. Now, I just don't know. I guess I'll have to go back to the Colonel..." Emerson's voice trailed away again.

Thomas got it instantly. Sergerant Emerson did not know this colonel and perhaps more importantly, the colonel did not know him. Colonel Sprague, killed so recently at Bull Run, had been Emerson's colonel. Now a new man, Colonel Rogers commanded. Emerson did not want to be the man who took a seemingly settled problem back to the colonel.

An interesting thought poked itself into Thomas Henderson's mind. As was his wont, he then proceeded to act before he had thoroughly considered all the facts.

"I have a solution for you. Mister Emerson." he promised. "Why don't I take responsibility for getting Mr. Bunten here to his new home? I'll take him to the Foundling Home for the short run and then I will look into this aunt matter. I'm from New York, I'll use my contacts to get to the bottom of this." He paused to gauge Emerson's reaction to his suggestion. "I'll be heading back into town later today, after I make a few stops," Henderson pushed on "and I can wrap this whole thing up. What do you say to that?"

Emerson wanted to take Henderson up on his offer, but he hesitated. Would it be proper? Would it be right? He looked down at his charge.

"What do you think, Jake?"

Jacob looked at Henderson and then at Emerson. "All to the good by me, Sergeant."

Emerson considered. He did like Henderson, so that gave him an out. "Are you sure, Thomas? I mean that's a big step."

"Not a step at all, I assure you. He'll ride with me this afternoon as I make my last call and then I'll take him to St. Anne's. Then I'll be glad to look into his situation. We'll find out where Banty here belongs!"

That was all the information the large Sergerant needed. It was decided. Thomas steadied his horse, while Emerson picked up Jacob and placed him behind Henderson. He helped untie the rope around the boy's waist and used it to tie the boy's haversack on the saddle. When that was done, the transaction was complete.

"I appreciate this, Thomas", Emerson said, offering his hand. "Babysittin' an urchin is not part of my job."

"Glad to help, Sergerant." Henderson said, shaking the offered hand. "The boy'll take a ride with me today and by tonight will be snuggly in his new lodgings." He looked at Emerson. "Of course, Sergerant, should you learn of any news, or details, I hope you will remember me."

"I will indeed, Thomas. You never know what you'll hear around an army camp. You never know at all and I do know how to reach you."

"Then with that Sergerant, we'll make our goodbyes. We have places to go. Ready boy?" Without waiting for Jake's answer, Henderson spurred the horse. "Good-bye Sergeant Emerson, I'm off to talk to a general!" Turning the horse's head, he waved goodbye over his shoulder. The two rode out of the camp.

Chapter 2

Henderson, with his brand new companion bouncing right behind him, headed southwest out of Camp Sprague. He wasn't exactly sure where he was going, but he had a decent idea of the general direction.

Thomas and the boy rode in an uncomfortable silence. Then Thomas said, "So tell me Banty…"

"Jacob." came the instant reply. A pause and then, "It's Jacob. Not Banty."

Henderson rode on a bit more. Then he gave a small nod and said "Very well. Let me try again. Tell me, Jacob, why were you so all-fired ready to ride off with a perfect stranger when you were nice and safe with the Second Rhode Island?"

Jacob answered in the artificially sweet tone he had used before. "Well, of course, Sir, I was very pleased to have the chance to accompany such an important man. Why you rode right through the camp while not even in uniform. You were recognized and respected, and I instantly knew you must be a very important person. A scout perhaps? I mean of man of such stature…"

This time Thomas was the one who did the interrupting. "Put away the soft soap, boy. I know that tone. Used it myself. Many a time. I'm sure not taking that malarkey from you!"

They rode on wordlessly for a few more minutes before Thomas asked, "Now, want to try that answer again?"

Jacob decided that he didn't really want to try to. He decided to stonily ignore Thomas instead.

Not hearing an answer, Henderson glanced back over his shoulder. "Or perhaps you'd like me to answer for you?"

Sulking, Jacob replied, "I'm sure I don't know what you mean!"

Henderson snorted, "Like hell! Well, here's how I see it. You figure your odds of getting away from one man are a lot better than getting away from a whole camp. Besides you were just this far from getting placed in a home. So I was your ticket out of camp as you saw it and then it would be a quick goodbye to me as you made your dash away." He turned back toward Jacob, giving him a smart alec smile. "Something like that, perhaps?"

"Dang!!" Jacob thought. Of course that was it. But he was surprised the man had cut to it so quickly. Jacob had not wanted to go to any orphanage, so getting on Thomas' horse seemed like a great way to at least temporarily avoid that fate. And it had occurred to him that it might be easier getting away from this younger gentleman than the experienced Sergeant Emerson. It would certainly be easier now that he was no longer tied up. But he had not expected Henderson to put all this together so quickly! The man was exactly right. But Jacob could surely not could not admit that, not at all. In fact, Jacob did not see anything he could say that would not hurt his cause, so he decided to return to silence. He would say nothing at all.

Henderson rode on for a few more minutes before asking "Nothing to add, nothing to say? Proverbial cat got your tongue? Humph!"

Still Jacob stayed silent, so Henderson did the same.

The quiet gave Thomas time to think. A feeling of unease had been creeping in. He was starting to believe that he had made a fairly large error. Once again, it seemed, he had acted rashly. He had certainly wanted to get on the Sergeant's good side. The Sergeant was a fine source of information, and goodness knows, he needed that. But was it a good bargain? Here he suddenly was riding through potentially enemy territory with a boy perched on his horse - a boy that he didn't even know. A lament began ringing in his head, "Oh, what have I gotten myself into?"

Thomas next began thinking about how he was going to get out of this mess.

At first, he thought he should turn right around and head back into the capital. Ride right up to St. Anne's and drop the little ragamuffin off. End of story. But that would cost him a day's work, and it would cost him potential information. Much as he may be ready to say goodbye to Mr. Jacob Bunten, he was not ready to turn his back on information. Information led to stories and stories led to paydays. No information meant no payday and that was something Thomas could not tolerate. No, he could not afford to waste the day. He could not be returning to the nation's capital without some new information for a story.

Thomas knew; he knew beyond a shadow of a doubt that he needed a story. Re-hashing a bunch of old facts would not make an article that would be printed in the New York *Constitutionalist*. Not only that, he knew that a weak effort would probably cost him his job. No job, no money, and no money meant…well, he didn't want to think about that.

But he had to think about it. He had to face reality. No income would mean Thomas would have to go home and that was something he deeply dreaded. Thomas did not want to return home.

Thomas had been born in New York City. His family had been in the New York City area for over one hundred years. During those years, almost the Henderson men had gone into some part of the medical field. Some as doctors, some as surgeons, some as teachers but all into medicine. His own father was one of the very first surgeons at that new New York City hospital, Bellevue. Why, when Thomas was born, his father exclaimed triumphantly, "I have a son! And the world has another doctor!"

The only problem with that was that Thomas had no interest in becoming a doctor. Not the first interest in becoming a doctor, surgeon or anything else that had any thing to do with the field of medicine. He had absolutely no desire to be in medicine. If the truth be told, well, the sight of blood didn't make him sick, he just believed blood was better off in the body and away from him. A career in medicine just was not going to happen - unless his family found a way to force him into the fold. Seeking to avoid that, from a relatively early age, Thomas had begun plotting his escape from New York City and the dreaded field of medicine.

To his immense surprise and delight, his plan had worked-so far. Thomas did not attack the idea of becoming a doctor with his family. Instead, he attacked the idea of going to college in New York, or anyplace near it for that. He did his research and came up with a list of prominent schools away from New York. With some effort, he began to show his parents that there were quality colleges south of New York.

He had finally, after much cajoling, convinced his parents that one, the College of William and Mary was an excellent choice. Started a mere few years after Harvard, it had famous instructors like George Wythe, and famous students like Thomas Jefferson.

Jefferson may have tipped the scales. If it was good enough for Jefferson after all, and so on. His family agreed that he could attend William and Mary to study medicine. Thomas was thrilled. He immediately agreed to go south, he just did not openly agree to study medicine. So it was a slightly surprised but happy student that found himself in Williamsburg, Virginia, in the fall of 1858.

William and Mary was a delight for Thomas. He took immediately to southern Virginia. The weather was wonderful. No more brutal New York winters. No more overcrowded, dirty, stinking city. The campus was beautiful, full of flowering trees and plants that he'd never seen before and certainly could not name.

The people he met were wonderful. They were educated, polite, respectful, civilized. Civilized. Of course there was one topic of conversation that never came up and one large group of people that Thomas never interacted with.

Thomas went to class, and did well; he was an intelligent young man. He was a dutiful son, writing home on a regular basis. He didn't exactly beg for additional funds, but he made it clear every red cent was sincerely appreciated. His parents wrote back, assuring him they missed him. The bank drafts arrived and Thomas could not have been more happy. Life was good.

Then, almost suddenly, the wheels had fallen off the wagon. Looking back, Thomas could barely believe so much had changed so quickly. Virginia, his temporarily adopted state, had voted to leave the Union. Leave the United States of America! Thomas was astonished and befuddled. How did this happen?

Of course, Thomas wasn't totally in the dark about the situation. There was always crazy talk coming from some source or other: Southern Rights, Northern Intrusion, Our Way of Life, etc. The state of South Carolina, and yes, it seemed like the entire state was always railing about something. What was that line he had heard in Williamsburg's Frog Pond tavern? Oh yes, "South Carolina, too little to be a republic, too big to be an insane asylum." Empty talk. Thomas and most of his Virginian friends had ignored it and their pleasant lives had continued.

Then, sudden madness! The world turned upside down. Crazy John Brown had tried to free the slaves at Harper's Ferry, failed miserably, and ended up hanged. Slavery hating Abraham Lincoln was elected president- without a single southern vote. And then seven southern states had up and left the Union! They were going to start their own country, The Confederate States of America, whatever that meant. No one could get a firm grip on the situation. Studious young men found ways to spend long hours in the taverns, seriously discussing the issues, at least as they understood them.

Sitting in a slave state, Thomas had assumed that almost all those around him would support the Confederacy. He was surprised to find so much disagreement about what should happen. Many speakers assured their audiences that "Lincoln, though a crackpot, was no real danger. They should all, South Carolina included, just settle down and let things get back to normal."

Others disagreed as vehemently as they could. "The North had abused the South since the Constitution was ratified. Southern states thought they were joining a confederation of states where their voices would matter. Instead, radicals in the North have taken over, literally designing plans to bankrupt their Southern neighbors. No Sir, it is certainly time to leave."

Thomas actually found himself strangely torn. Intellectually, Thomas did not have a problem with the southern states leaving the country. They had voluntarily agreed to join their sister states in creating the Union; why would they not have the same right to leave? Free to come, free to leave was the way he saw it. That was just plain common sense for Thomas. If states were leaving, fine. But that did not mean Thomas could leave with them.

As much as he loved Virginia, he could never leave the United States. And he could never be a part of this new Confederacy. The Confederacy's founding fathers, from day one, had made it clear that slavery was the reason their new country existed. Confederate Vice President Alexander Stephens had called slavery the new country's cornerstone. That one single issue made all the difference. And truthfully, recently, the concept of slavery had become extremely real to him. When he first came to Virginia, he hadn't really given slavery much thought. There weren't that many slaves in New York, and certainly none that he knew. He was much more likely to run into an abolitionist than a slave.

But in his two years in Virginia, he had found the practice unavoidable. He had quickly seen first hand the evils of slavery. It troubled him so much that people he truly enjoyed had no problem owning and mistreating other people.Thomas could never support a nation founded on the belief that slavery was a God-given right. Thomas had loved his time in the South; he had come to admire many people. But he could never ignore the despicable nature of slavery. Thomas would never live in the Confederacy.

In the early days of the turmoil, secession had felt like an academic exercise, a debate in the common room among respectful friends. Leave the Union? Never! This was Virginia, after all. Virginia, state of Presidents. Home to George Washington, Thomas Jefferson, James Madison and James Monroe. Home to George Wythe, Richard Henry Lee, Patrick Henry, and Peyton Randolph. Virginia would never leave the Union! Never.

And yet, suddenly, there at the Mechanics Institute, right there on Capitol Hill in Richmond, a Virginia convention had come together to discuss the situation. Delegates from all over the state came to Richmond to meet and express their opinions. After much discussion, a vote was taken and Virginia had voted to remain in the Union. They voted to support slavery, (of course they did, thought Thomas) but they voted to remain in the Union. "As it should be!" Thomas assured his friends. Assuming the matter settled, his attention returned to his studies.

Then two months later, Thomas, and many others were stunned, astonished actually, when basically the same group of men reconvened and revoted. This time they voted to take Virginia right out of the United States! Looking back, Thomas believed there were two major events that changed their votes, two events that turned the men from using words to using bullets. The first was the attack on Fort Sumter, South Carolina. President Lincoln refused to abandon the fort to the Confederacy and the South, on April 04, 1861 opened an artillery barrage against the fort. Speeches had indeed turned into cannon fire.

The second catalyst was President Lincoln's reaction to that attack. He issued a proclamation calling for all loyal states to send their militias to put down the

Confederate rebellion. This put slave-holding Virginia in a terrible spot. Take up arms against their sister slave-holding states? People sadly shook their heads. They simply could not see that happening. Union support in both the convention and the state quickly melted away. When the vote was taken, secessionists carried the day. Virginia voted to leave the Union. The day after the vote, Northern troops marched out of Washington, D.C. and occupied the Virginia city of Alexandria. "Virginia is invaded! War is at hand!" screamed the headlines.

Northern voices countered that federal troops had merely moved from one place in the Union to another. Federal troops had been stationed in Virginia since the beginning of the country. Nothing had changed.

Back at William and Mary, Thomas felt as if the world had truly turned upside down. Suddenly, he no longer lived in the United States? Yet his day to day routine was virtually unchanged. Classes were held, exams were given, students groggily rose from bed, and at the end of the day, students went to bed. Life went on, well at least for the immediate future. The term was drawing to a close.

Outside the college routine however, things were dramatically changing. Men began to form military units and began drilling on the town's common. Talk of war dominated the town. People everywhere asked, "Would Virginia go alone, or join the new Confederacy? Was war inevitable?"

Personally, Thomas was in a very odd place. He did not want to live in the Confederacy; he would not live in a country solely built on slavery. He certainly would not join any Southern army defending that country. But he did not want to go home. He had no desire to be in New York. Nor did he want to join a northern army attempting to stop a southern army. He did not know what to do. So he did nothing and waited.

The school year drew to an end and students left Williamsburg for their various destinations. Plenty of Thomas' friends left intending to join the new Southern army. They were off to defend their new country and their way of life. Others left to join the Union forces. They would fight to preserve the Union. With regret, Thomas watched them all go. He had the deep worry they were all making a tragic mistake. And still, he could not find his place.

Then came another bolt of news. The Virginia Convention had voted to join the Confederacy. That turned the tide for Thomas. He could no longer live in Virginia. He would not live in the Confederacy.

But where to go? Home seemed his only choice. Then a thought came to him. Why not move north to Washington, D.C? Why not move to the nation's capital and see what was going on for himself? "Yes, why not? It's only 150 miles or so north, and north is the direction I need to go." With virtually no more thought or plan than that, Thomas found himself riding away from his adopted home. "Goodbye, Williamsburg, I have no idea when or if I will ever see you again." With a bit of money left in his pocket, a very little bit, Thomas floated north on the tides of war-fever.

Thomas was astonished by what he found in Washington. He fell in love with the city instantly. The city was a swirling cauldron of action and activity. Troops were everywhere, bustling every which way. It was even hard to walk on the streets, every inch was full. Every hotel room was full, every boarding house. Thomas was lucky to find a temporary bunk in a barn-like building behind a house in Georgetown. He shared the barn with six other men. He was forced to share his bed with one (and a very smelly one too, as Thomas forcefully told everyone who would listen.)

Thomas wandered the city, taking it all in, trying to make sense of it all. It was so outside his world, such a change from sleepy Williamsburg. People swirled everywhere, in every direction, at every hour. Thomas was from New York. He knew all about great cities. But he was not prepared for Washington, D.C. Endless rumors pulsed on war-charged electricity. Everyone who was anyone, or anyone who wanted to be someone, was here. Stand for a minute and watch colonels, majors, generals, senators, representatives, ambassadors hurry by. Why Thomas had even walked by the White House and seen the great man himself. This was certainly the center for the struggle for America.

Rumors were rampant. Thomas had heard it all in the short time he'd been in town. 'The Great Southern Army (and where had that term or that army come from Thomas asked himself?) was reportedly moving up from Virginia to occupy the capital. Rebel flags flew across the river! (And amazing enough, that was true, Thomas saw them for himself. Though instead of flying at the head of invading troops, it looked like they flew from private Virginian homes. Virginia, that other country was just across the Potomac after all.) No more Union troops were to be allowed through Maryland. Thousands of Union troops were pushing down from Maryland right this instant, clearing a bloody path through the state.' The rumors never stopped. Thomas loved it. He loved it all.

Except for the smell. He hated that. The putrid smell of sewage, animal waste, and unwashed humans filled the air. Oh, and the food. He hated the food. It was atrocious. It was barely edible. No, that's not true. It was not edible! The slop they had the nerve to put in front of a person. And the cost for that slop! Sadly, everything had suddenly become sky-high expensive; prices were soaring through the roof! He hated that! His coins were flowing from his purse at an alarming rate. After one rather late night on the town, Thomas cast his eyes at his threadbare purse and sadly realized he could not afford to stay in the nation's capital for long, sharing a bed in a barn or not.

Another thing eating at Thomas was his home situation. He had written his parents when he had decided to leave William and Mary. He had told them he was making his way north, but he had warned that things were very uncertain right now, so he had no idea when he would arrive anywhere! He promised that he would keep them posted, which, of course, he had not done. He had sent a note north once he had arrived in D.C. but he had not explained that he had no plans to come home. His last word north was a short telegraph, promising them he was fine but adding nothing else. He knew he could not hide from them forever. As if his guilty conscience wasn't enough, his declining fortunes really brought that fact home.

Thomas knew of no way to get more money. Of course, he could seek employment, but it seemed that every single person he met was looking for a job, an appointment, a commission. And Thomas did not really have any marketable skills. What job, exactly, would he be asking for? What could he do? His mood darkened as the days passed. The days passed; his pennies continued to disappear.

Then, a chance meeting with a fellow New Yorker changed everything. Thomas really should not have even agreed to the engagement. A few of his fellow "Barn Rats", as they had taken to calling each other, had decided to try a new place in town, Ebbitts Grill. The budget did not really allow it, but "a man has to eat," Thomas told himself. He agreed to go. They were seated, ready for a libation (or so), a bit of food, and hopefully a night full of gossip and news.

That's when Thomas spotted a face he knew. He couldn't instantly pull the name. He began working backward in his mind. He wasn't from the college nor from Williamsburg… and then Thomas had it. He was up and out of his chair before he even knew it. "Elihu Randolph Pitt! " he called loudly, walking toward the man.

The man turned, searching the crowded room. He saw Thomas and smiled, "Thomas Henderson! Why, what in the world...? What are you doing here in the nation's capital?"

Elihu was a friend from New York. Elihu had gone to school with Thomas and their families had traveled in the same circles. The two happily exchanged hearty handshakes, and some back slapping. "You must join me, Thomas!" Elihu insisted. Thomas quickly agreed. He excused himself from the Barn Rats and began catching up with Elihu .

The two soon found they were in similar situations, although Elihu was clearly in better straits. Like Thomas, the war had drawn him to the capital, but unlike Thomas, he had a job, a commission if you will.

"I have been employed," he said, drawing out the words and sticking his thumbs into his vest, "to recruit writers for the New York *Constitutionalist*." His chest puffed out as he spoke.

"The what?!" Thomas asked.

"It's a new newspaper back home," Elihu explained. "Mister Alpheus R. Comstock - the R. stands for Reginald - is the owner and editor. He is committed to fully telling the story of this war to the folks back home. So he is looking for people who can provide him with information and stories about the war. Thomas," he said, leaning forward and staring Thomas straight in the eyes, "unlike most folks, he figures we are in for a terrible fight."

Thomas leaned back. "Well, I don't know about that..." he said thinking of all the talk he had heard back in Virginia about a quick and easy victory for the South, "but what does that have to do with you?"

"Well, exactly! When he learned that I had a hankering to go south and see some of this action, Mr. Comstock made me a proposal. So here it is. He needs information about what's going on. He needs a lot of information, and he needs it in a timely fashion. So my job is to find qualified folks to provide him with that information."

"What kind of information?" Thomas asked.

"Everything!" Elihu enthusiastically answered. "Everything! What's happening with the troops, what's happening with the politicians? What are the people saying? What are the troops saying? What's the mood of of the country? Mr. Comstock needs everything you can provide so the people back home can understand what's going on with this war!"

"So I'd be a reporter for the *Constitutionalist*, then?"

Elihu paused, "Well, no, not exactly. He has a different vision. He wants researchers and folks to write up that research. Then he'll turn those reports into articles for our readers."

Thomas leaned back in, "So he will pay me to write?" This suddenly sounded very interesting.

Elihu held his hands palms out toward Thomas. "Hold on, hold on! Let's not get ahead of ourselves here. First we are looking for college graduates; we want men who know how to research and write."

"Well, that's me!" Thomas instantly responded. "Proud new graduate of the fine school, the College of William and Mary!"

(Inside his head the preacher side of his brain suddenly perked up. "New graduate? When did that happen?" "Not now!" the pragmatic side of Thomas' brain pushed back.)

"Tell me more!" Thomas continued.

"We're looking for candidates from all over the country. He figures the war will be in the south, the west, at sea, heck, it may even come north. He's willing to hire researchers all around the country. And as you're a New York man with southern experience, you'll be perfect. I'm sure you have all kinds of connections and angles." Elihu decided to push the issue. "When can you start?"

"So he'll pay for every word I write?" Thomas asked, returning to the pertinent subject.

"Almost," came the reply, "he'll pay for every word he publishes."

"Hmmmm," Thomas muttered, "that takes a bit of the bloom off the rose." The job suddenly looked just a bit less wonderful.

"But he'll pay a stipend and advance you some expense money," his friend countered. "Not a big stipend and the advance will be taken out of your pay, but it's a job, and it gets you started." He paused and sank the hook a bit deeper. "And it's coins in your purse, starting tonight! So what do you say?"

Thomas would have liked more money and more security, but since it was his best and truthfully only offer, he accepted. He found himself suddenly "affiliated" with the New York *Constitutionalist,* a newspaper he had previously never heard of.

His acquaintance enthusiastically shook his hand. "Now just one last word," he said as downed his drink, "you are not the only associate the *Constitutionalist* has in this area. Your job is to be the best!" He patted Thomas on the shoulder. "Tell you what, we'll meet tomorrow, and I'll give you all the details on filing your stories - and getting paid! How's that?"

He stopped to pull a watch from his vest pocket. "Well, I must be away. I have an engagement." His watch disappeared and his purse came out. "But first," he said, opening his purse, "Here is your advance. " He dropped several coins in Thomas' hand. "Now you need to start thinking about possible stories!"

Later that evening, a few drinks to the worse, Thomas made his way back to the Barn. He was employed. He had money in his pocket. He had a future. He was staying in D.C. He was going to do important work. He dropped into bed with his smelly bedmate and thought no more about anything.

The next day, Thomas, with a queasy stomach and headache, turned up at Elihu"s lodgings. It quickly became clear that it wasn't a job as much as it was an opportunity. The paper had access to a telegraph wire, quite the new technology and that was impressive. Everyone was to submit their copy over the wire. The editor would pick and choose and the winning contributor would be paid by the published word. Still lacking a better opportunity, Thomas plunged into the work. He traveled the city and made as many contacts as he could. He wanted those words published.

His first key contact turned out to be a sergeant in the Second Rhode Island Infantry. When the war broke out, the Second Rhode Island was one of the first regiments to arrive in the capital. One evening, playing a friendly game of poker with a group of New York boys, Thomas met Sergeant Emerson of Rhode Island. Thomas set to work losing and soon he and Sergeant Emerson were firm friends, for that evening at least.

It might have been a temporary friendship, but Thomas had wrangled an invitation to visit the Second Rhode Island camp. Things went well, and Thomas was soon repeatedly returning to the Second Rhode Island camp. It was a brand new world for all, and Thomas drank it in. He was astonished how much information lay "lying around" as he put it. He heard information about the Union forces that astonished him. He wrote inches and inches of newspaper column. Thomas wrote but it was to no avail. Not one inch had yet seen the light of day. Thomas remained unpublished and unpaid.

On another front he had contacted his family. Now that he was employed, he felt much better about sharing his situation. He did not provide many details, for instance it slipped his mind to share that he was living in a barn, but he did otherwise bring them up to date. He wanted them to know he was firmly out of Virginia, employed (barely), and healthy. He dreaded sending the letter, but he knew he had to. He owed them that much and truthfully much more, but for now this letter would have to do.

He was very surprised to receive his father's reply. No, to be honest, he was stunned. His father said he understood why he had left college and said he was pleased Thomas was not in the army. He was also pleased that his son was making a positive contribution to the North's efforts. "Stay out of harm's way, contribute to the Northern Cause; and there will be plenty of time to return to the study of medicine. This struggle must be won by the North and your efforts will help that victory. Surely it will be a quick and sudden fight and all will once again be right with the world." Unwritten was the acknowledgement that Thomas would also be out of the army.

Thomas was surprised. How would his efforts help the Northern cause? (especially if he did not get published.) What was his father saying? "Stay out of harm's way" was a generic thing to say to a son in troubled times. But should Thomas be doing more? Should he be in uniform? It was a persistent, nagging thought, a tooth that ached, something that never quite left him. Still, he was not ready to join the Union army. Too much still troubled him.

Much more troubled him after the events of July 16-21, 1861. Those events changed Thomas forever. It changed a great many other people as well.

The pressure had been on for a Northern attack on the Confederate army. The Rebels were encamped a mere 30 some miles southwest of the capital, creating a barrier between Washington and Richmond, Virginia, the new capital of the Confederate States. "On to Richmond" became the northern rallying cry. General McDowell, commander of the Union forces, was compelled to move his army of volunteers south. He had protested that his men were too green and the president himself had agreed, but he had also countered that they, meaning the Rebels, were green too. The order to proceed had been given.

And that order had spread all over D.C., or it seemed to Thomas. Everyone seemed to know the Union Army was on the march to Manassas. One of the regiments moving was the Second Rhode Island. Thomas used his ties to the regiment to attach himself to their shirttails as they left the capital.

He immediately submitted the story of his departure to the *Constitutionalist*. As he left town, he wondered if they would publish it.

The march had commenced at the unbelievable hour of 3:00 a.m. "It's darker than the inside of a cow!" Thomas complained to Emerson. But when ordered, they marched dark or not. They soon fell into an odd pattern. They marched, they stopped, they marched, they slowed, they marched, they stopped. The road to Manassas seemed to be infinitely long, but Thomas was excited. He rode right along with the regiment. He was heading to battle. Of course, he was worried. He was extremely worried about getting his story published. Who wouldn't be worried about that? Would the telegraph be available? Would another researcher beat him to the story?

Like so many, he rode with quiet confidence. He expected to have a pleasant ride to Manassas (after all everyone knew where the army was heading.) The rebels were outnumbered. One Yankee beat ten Rebels. The Union had the regular forces. The Rebels would run for miles. The war would be over in a week. Putting the Rebellion down in one fell swoop was how he thought about it. Like so many others, he worried that the whole war would end before he got there. Then where would he be? What if he missed all the fun?

Interestingly, Thomas did not remember that he had heard these same comments from his Confederate-supporting classmates. They, of course, had put a slightly different slant on things.

Strangely, not only soldiers were making their way to Manassas. By day two, crowds of picnickers and sightseers had joined the march. Civilians, all intent on seeing the destruction of the Rebels, came for the fun. How bad could it be if people were bringing picnics? The mood was light. Ladies twirled their parasols and chatted as their carriages carried them merrily toward the upcoming fight.

That light mood quickly evaporated however when everyone, Thomas included, found out exactly how disastrous it could be. The Rebels had been watching the Union march from D.C. They watched as the army made its way toward Manassas. Just as the civilians had known where the army was marching, so had the Rebels. They watched as the Second Rhode Island approached Matthew's Hill. Those hidden Rebels waited patiently until the Rhode Island men had moved into position. Then, all hell broke loose. The First Louisiana opened up with an artillery attack and sudden death and destruction rained down on the Union troops.

When the first Rebel cannon fired, Thomas was seated on his horse, a few yards behind the line of men. He was instantly terrified. The sound was deafening. He had never heard anything remotely like this. Then the shell landed, and he forgot all about the noise. His world changed forever.

Thomas was suddenly engulfed in a deadly maelstrom. He had never seen, felt, heard, nor imagined such a hell. No matter where he turned, he could not escape. The ground shook; the cannons thundered. Man after man fell where they stood, where he stood. Waves of dense smoke removed all his points of reference. He was completely surrounded by unimaginable death and destruction. He suddenly knew he was going to die, and he was terrified.

"Whoosh!" a force screamed past his ear. He turned to see a cannonball bounce once and then strike a Rhode Island boy right in the leg. The ball ripped right through the knee and kept on bouncing right through the man behind the Rhode Island soldier. Thomas watched, horrified and mesmerized as the soldier's black boot started spinning through the air. Thomas realized, as a wave of vomit rose, that the bottom half of the soldier's leg was still in the spinning boot. The bloody top half was hanging from the stunned boy's torso. For a minute the boy stood there as if he could not believe what had happened to him. Then he died.

Thomas half fell, half jumped from his horse. He collapsed on the ground. He lay there, retching uncontrollably. He vomitted until there were nothing left. Still his stomach spasmed. The unending artillery barrage from hell continued.

The image of that spinning leg would not leave his head. He didn't know it at the time, but that image would be with him for a long, long time. The horror, the sound, the fury, the death, the smoke, the noise all rolled over him,

Thomas tried to bury himself, literally tried to make himself disappear. He closed his eyes, determined not to see one more second of the carnage. If he couldn't see it, perhaps this incredible destruction was not occurring. Thomas never knew how long he lay on the ground cowering. He honestly did not care.

Eventually, (minutes, hours, days?) a realization came to Thomas. The shelling had stopped. And then slowly, very slowly, a second realization came to Thomas. He realized he was alive, and he realized the cannon fire had ended. He began to slowly move his hands around his body, searching. He patted his arms, legs and trunk, searching for wounds. Amazingly enough, he found none.

Crawling, stumbling, retching, and crying he pushed himself up. The screams of the wounded and dying, the crash of still on-going rifle fire filled his ears. The hell of the battle continued though the Rebels had withdrawn their cannon.

For the rest of his long life, he never understood how he survived. By all odds, he most certainly should have died. He did not. He was, for the moment, safe. The immediate battle had moved away from the Second Rhode Island.

Later he found out that newly arriving Union troops, led by Colonel William T. Sherman, helped turn the

Confederate's line. The Confederates fell back toward Henry's Hill. The battle moved away from Matthews Hill, away from the Second Rhode Island and away from Thomas Henderson.

Thomas rose from the ground with one thought - "FLEE! GET OUT OF HERE!" His entire body, from his ringing ears to his burning eyes, screamed at him, "Escape!" He didn't care about the army, he didn't care about reporting, he didn't care about getting any story, he cared about living.

Then, he saw his chance. Through the swirling smoke a riderless horse came cantering toward him. He jumped to grab the flopping reins. He didn't know whose horse it was, and he didn't care. He knew he was stealing a horse, and he couldn't have cared less.

Thomas swung into the saddle. He was alive and suddenly, he saw a way to stay that way. Minutes before, he was sure he was dead. Now he threw himself on the horse and tried to claw his way out of the madness. He had to ride away from this hatred, death, and carnage. He had to get to safety! He had to save himself! It was the only thought he had.

He dug his knees and heels into the horse. In a complete state of shock, he rode away from the carnage. Later he would not even remember getting on the horse. At that minute his entire life was devoted to the idea of escape. He had to escape the blood, the screams, the carnage, the destruction. His senses reeled. He kept seeing that boot spinning through the air.

The words didn't actually form in his head, but he knew that he never, never ever wanted to see any battle again. He didn't want to see another person die, never wanted to hear another shell scream. He knew his life had changed forever this day.

He did ride away from the battle. He found himself riding north, back toward D.C. As he rode away, realizing he was going to survive, another thought began crossing his mind. "But I'll do my job." he began to repeat woodenly. "I'll tell the others about this madness!" He was getting away from this agony and he would file his story.

Strangely enough, that was what happened. He'd ridden away from the battle, following the crowds of panicked picnickers, and actually made it to the telegraph station. Evidently he filed a story.

He never remembered doing a single minute of any of it. He didn't remember riding back to D.C., he didn't remember writing a single word and he surely didn't remember putting his story on the wire.

He did remember, however, that no story of his was published. In fact, no word came from New York City at all. He later on wondered exactly what he had sent. It probably was amazing he was still allowed to use the wire.

The *Constitutionalist* published a story written by another researcher. It was a coherent story accurately describing the terrible battle. Thomas could not have written it. It was no wonder his story was not published.

Thomas later admitted to himself in the dark hours of the night that his story should have been rejected. He really did not remember what he put into the telegraph. Considering his state of mind at the time, it might have been gibberish. It might not have been English.

But the stories that were published stunned and shocked a nation, North and South both. How could there be so much bloodshed on both sides? This destroyed so many of the myths that had filled the air. So much for the easy win, so much for the "On to Richmond" cries. So much for the promises that Yankees could not hurt southern gentlemen! Thomas could not help but remember the quote of Alabamian LeRoy Pope Walker. Walker had promised, that if war did erupt, he would bring his handkerchief along to soak up the entire amount of blood that would be shed. "Tell me, Sir," Thomas wanted to ask, "how big is your handkerchief?" For Thomas had seen buckets, no, gallons shed that day. No, Mister LeRoy Pope Walker, there was no doubt that this was going to be a very bloody, very serious war.

But Thomas had enough problems of his own without worrying about Alabama's Mr. Walker. He was back in Washington, D.C., currently sleeping in a barn and he was not even guaranteed that. He had the bed until his money ran out. The remaining coins in his pocket had to feed him and bed him. When they were gone, he was destitute. He had no way to purchase food to keep him alive. Was he to beg? He was not in college nor would he be returning to William and Mary for apparently a good long time. Was he to go home? He shuddered at the thought. He had no job. He had sent some gibberish that had not been published. He was sure he was on very thin ice with his employer. Thin ice, heck, he may well be fully under the ice, freezing to death as far as he knew. Of course he could try to find another job here in D.C., but what would that be exactly?

There was a bit of good news. His bed mate, Mister Smelly himself, had disappeared. Moved on? Moved out? Thomas did not care; he had a bed to himself and that was a step up. Lying in that bed, Thomas did some serious thinking. He did not want to go home, but he did not see another job coming. It seemed he had no choices; so he decided he had to learn to successfully do the job he had signed on for. He knew he did not currently know how to successfully do that job, so it was time to go to figure it out. He committed to learning this "reporting stuff" and staying in D.C.

He set up a plan. To write a story he needed information. To get information, he needed sources. He needed a new plan. So he scratched out a plan of action and set about to put in place. Taking small steps, he would create a job. He would become a contributing member to the New York *Constitutionalist*. He would stand on his own two feet.

And that was why he had ridden into the Second Rhode Island's camp looking for information. And that was why he was now riding across the Virginia countryside. It was time to become a reporter.

Chapter 3

After an hour or so of steady riding, they came to the newly constructed, or perhaps it was more accurate to say, still being constructed, Camp Corcoran. As they approached the closed gate, Thomas unconsciously touched his haversack. He hoped the papers inside would serve as his entry pass to this new camp. Truth be told, Thomas was nervous. He had no idea if these papers would work. The full extent of Thomas' rough plan was to try to use the papers to meet Lieutenant Colonel Webb. And if that didn't work? If they were rejected? What would happen to the two of them? Would they face arrest? Would they be accused of being spies? "Don't go down that road!" Thomas sternly told himself. He thrust the unwelcome thoughts aside.

But other nagging thoughts quickly boiled up. What had he been thinking when he agreed to take Jacob? He remembered all the times people told him he went off "half cocked." Well here was another pretty good example of that! What a mistake he had made.

But, perhaps, just perhaps, it was a mistake that could be rectified. Perhaps it was a mistake that could he could even take care of quickly. He worked the idea around in his mind. Maybe this whole thing would be shortly over. Perhaps, Thomas thought hopefully, Jacob will just carry out his plan. Perhaps all Thomas had to do was stay out of his way. Thomas gave his hat a tug, seating it more firmly on his head. He rode on toward the camp.

And then a jab of, what, responsibility? unexpectedly hit Thomas. After all, hadn't he promised the sergeant that he would take Jacob to the foster home?

"On the other hand," Henderson's practical side countered, "did the sergeant even care? Once the sergeant handed him off, he'd probably washed his hands of the whole situation. And anyway what if I did drop him off at the orphanage? What kind of a life would he have there?"

Henderson's more responsible side countered right back "Yeah, and what kind of a life will it be for a child deserted in a half-built army camp? You expect him to make his own way?"

Henderson angrily shook his head, trying to end his inner conversation.

Thomas was not the only one thinking about the future. Jacob was peering eagerly over Henderson's shoulder. His eagerness, however, soon gave way to apprehension. He was not pleased with his first impressions. "Wow!" he thought, "Things are different!" As they rode closer, Jacob began to become worried. This camp was not like the ones he had hidden in earlier.

Camp Corcoran wasn't a finished camp by any means. Half-built wooden structures stood among piles of Virginia clay. Raw trenches ran in multiple directions. Even half-built though it was clear from his first glance that this camp was much different than the Washington, D.C. camps he knew. For one thing this camp was more organized - and much more structured. Inside the walls, he could see soldiers marching. A bugle sounded orders. Right outside the main gate, entrenched batteries stood ready to repel Confederate attack. And at those gates, those gates they had to pass, guards stood at attention, ready to challenge all newcomers.

"Those guards have to know they are guarding piles of clay," thought Jacob, "but they look like they are guarding the White House." He shook his head, "Way different this time around."

Before Bull Run the camps Jacob knew were as open as the door to his pa's general store. People seemingly came and went as they pleased. In many places, it was almost hard to see where the camp ended and the city began.

And that had made it easy to be one small figure lurking about. Back then, no one paid attention to a single child. As he examined Camp Corcoran, Jacob began to worry that this was no longer the case.

As it turned out, he was right to worry. Before Thomas could even ride up to the gate, one of the guards stepped forward to block their progress. As he moved, he shifted his musket from the rest position to ready to use. In a polite but certainly not friendly tone, he half shouted, "Yes, Sir! How may I help you?"

Thomas pulled the horse to a halt and glanced at the soldier's rank. "Afternoon, Corporal."

The guard made no reply. He stared stonily at Thomas.

"Ahem," Thomas quickly said, "I have some identification right here." Thomas opened the sack and pulled out two papers. "I'm Thomas Henderson of the New York *Constitutionalist*," he said, handing his first paper to the soldier. "And I'm here to see Lieutenant Colonel Webb." he finished, handing his second paper over. From the back of the horse came the whispered accusation, "Lieutenant Colonel? But you told Sergeant Emerson…"

"Later, Jacob, later!" Thomas whispered back, waving the boy's comments away.

Resting his musket, the guard looked both papers over closely. "These seem to be in order, Sir," he said handing them back, "I'm afraid you missed Colonel Webb, though."

"Oh?"

"He was through earlier, much earlier. I would be very surprised to find him still here." He passed the papers back to Thomas. "But of course, I may be mistaken. You are welcome to ride back to headquarters and find out" he said.

He reshouldered the musket and swung aside.

Thomas gave a half wave, half salute and spurred his horse through the opening gate. He instantly felt like a fool. "What kind of motion was that?" he sternly asked himself. "Want to fully convince these people you're a fraud and an idiot?"

The truth was Thomas was as nervous as the cat in the room with the rocking chairs. He had not been sure at all that those papers would have gotten him past the guard. They might well not get him past the next one. He was absurdly relieved the guard had not asked him about his position with the *Constitutionalist*. Thomas had given that question thought and was ready to embellish as much as needed. He wasn't quite ready to claim to be the owner of the paper, but outside of that...

He was also nervous about meeting Lieutenant Colonel Webb. It was true that he had a letter from him, but that letter was a simple politeness, not an invitation. How would Webb react when Thomas rode up? He had not granted Thomas an interview. He had not even said he would meet him.

Still Thomas and Jacob rode on. Jacob swung his head from side to side attempting to take it all in. They rode past howitzers, barbette guns, field guns and marching soldiers. They rode past rows and rows of tents. The camp appeared to house hundreds of soldiers. Men moved with a sense of purpose. There was no lying about, no lallygagging.

Jacob felt his plan evaporate as they rode through the camp. He wasn't sliding into the background here. He'd stand out like a sore thumb in this camp. There was no place for him at Camp Corcoran. Unconsciously, he settled himself a little more securely behind Thomas.

They arrived at headquarters, a log cabin assembled among the piles of newly dug clay. They met another set of guards. This time they accepted Thomas' story without asking for papers. "Sorry, Sir," one guard said when Thomas announced his purpose. "I saw Colonel Webb ride out a good two hours ago."

A disappointed sigh. "Do you have any idea where he was heading?" Thomas asked hopefully.

"Well,.." came the drawled response. The man turned to his partner. "Any idea where Colonel Webb lit out to?"

"Might have been to Fort Ellsworth," ventured the second man.

"Fort Ellsworth?" came the first soldier's incredulous reply. "Why on God's earth would anyone go there? It's nothing but a pile of logs and stones. It's not nearly finished. Nothing on earth for the Colonel to do there!"

"You asked and I'm telling!" the man shot right back. "Where do you think he went?"

"I figure Fort Washington." came the satisfied reply.

"Fort Washington? Fort Washington? " blustered the other, "Why that's a good 15 to 18 miles from here!" Then he added as if to prove his point, "and it's across the Potomac!" He settled back on his heels as if that settled everything.

Thomas interrupted their dialogue. "Thank you gentlemen. Appreciate your help. We'll leave you to your day." He started to turn the horse's head and then paused. "Before I go, do you mind if I ask where you boys call home?"

"Wisconsin," came one reply. "New York" was the other. Henderson perked up at hearing that. "I'm a New Yorker! Where you from?"

"Elmira, Sir. Thirteenth New York Volunteers. "

"Second Wisconsin Volunteers," chimed in the other. "Under the command of General Sherman!"

Henderson nodded. "Elmira, a bit west of me. As is Wisconsin! Well, all the best to you gentlemen. We will seek Lieutenant Colonel Webb elsewhere." The soldiers saluted Henderson as he turned the horse toward the exit.

They rode out of the camp and Henderson pulled the horse into the shade of a tree.

"Well, Jacob, shall we try another camp?"

"Yes, Sir," came the quick reply.

Surprised at the quick, and polite answer, Thomas almost turned and gave the boy a look, but thought better of it. He rode on toward the southwest.

After a few more hours riding and a short stop to buy some milk, bread and a few early apples, the two arrived at Camp Whipple. Once again, surprisingly enough, the story and the papers worked again. The results were the same as well. "No Sir, you're a good two to three hours late. Colonel Webb has come and gone." This time there was no invitation to visit headquarters. But past the guards, the two could see inside the camp. Both saw that Camp Whipple bore a striking resemblance to Camp Corcoran. Again, neither camp was like the pre-Bull Run camps in Washington D.C.

By this time, the afternoon had slipped away. Thomas most certainly wanted to visit another camp but time was against him. He was debating a course of action when the decision was suddenly made for him. From the west came a low but insistent roll of thunder. A Virginian summer thunderstorm was on the way, and it was apparently headed for him. He quickly came to a decision.

This time he did turn back toward Jacob. "Listen here, Jacob. I know we had a deal and I was to take you to St. Anne's Foundling Home. But we're miles from there right now and as you can see and hear, we are going to get wet. In addition, I'd like to visit another camp tomorrow. What say you we find a place to spend the night, visit that camp tomorrow, and then I'll be happy to take you to St. Anne's?"

Jacob needed no time to answer. His first plan to slide away from Henderson at the earliest moment had proven impossible. His next plan was to avoid St. Anne's, so anytime spent out of D.C. was a good move.

"Yes, Sir, suits me fine."

Henderson cast a look at the weather. "I figure we've got an hour or so. Let's keep heading south and see what we can see." The skies darkened, the winds picked up, and the temperature dropped, but the rain held off as they pushed south. They did indeed make it another hour before Thomas pulled up next to a sign. "Collard's Sparrow," it read, pointing south. "It's time to find shelter," Thomas said as he spurred the horse, "On to Collard's Sparrow."

Collard's Sparrow, as it turned out, was not a town. It was not a village. It was a hill with a crumbling house and a partially torn-down barn. Neither had a roof, so they offered little in the way of shelter. Now they were in danger of losing the light, the rain was going to rip open at any time and they had no place to stay.

"This way, I think" mused Thomas. He headed off across a field.

"Any idea where you're going?" Jacob asked a bit sarcastically.

"Patience, son, patience. Someone farms these fields and if they farm, they have a farmhouse. Surely someone will offer shelter to two wandering pilgrims."

"Pilgrims? You mean like Plymouth Rock Pilgrims?" He made a show of looking around. "I don't claim to know everything about geography, but this does not look like Massachusetts to me!"

"Been to Massachusetts many times, have you?" Thomas shot back, but inside he was impressed by Jacob's comments. He adjusted his tone. "So you know about the Pilgrims, do you?"

Jacob straightened up. "I had some book learning. I've been working in Pa's store." He spoke to Thomas as if Thomas were a simpleton. "You can't work in a store and be un-educated, you know."

Henderson gave him a wry smile. "Why I do believe you are entirely correct, Jacob. No way to be uneducated and successful in a store at all!" Thomas then pointed at the horizon where they could make out the outline of a house and barn. "Shall we try our luck?"

A musket barrel and an angry "Get out! NOW!" greeted them at that first house. Pushing on, they tried two more with no more luck. Darkness was closing in and the rain was starting to come down.

"There's no town out here?" asked Jacob.

" Nope. Surprising, I know. This part of Alexandria County is mostly rural even though we are not that many miles from the capital." They pushed on.

At the fourth house a farmwife answered their hale. She also held a gun in her hand. "No room in the house," she flatly announced as soon as Thomas made his request. Fat rain drops were raising little puffs of dust as they fell into her barnyard. They fell a little faster with each passing second. The heavens were going to open soon.

"Would you deny a fellow Virginian shelter from the storm?" implored Thomas.

"Fellow Virginian? Not with that accent. You're not from Virginia!" came the instant reply.

"Oh, but dear madam, I am. You are absolutely correct, I started elsewhere, but the last years have seen me in nearby Williamsburg. And a beautiful town it is," Thomas said, waving his hand toward the southeast in the general direction of Williamsburg.

The farmwife hesitated and then made her decision. She swung the barrel toward the barn. "Since you've got your son with you, I reckon y'all can sleep in the barn. The house is full, but there's room in the hayloft."

Not bothering to correct her about their relationship, Thomas gave her a low bow, "Thank you much, dear lady!" he said, meaning it. "We will be gone in the morning."

"Now no smoking in that barn, no open flame. Can't risk it, hear?"

"Yes Ma'am, again our thanks."

"And remember," she called as Thomas and Jacob started toward the welcome shelter of the barn, "This here gun's protectin' this house!"

Thomas waved his agreement and they rushed into the barn out of the increasingly energetic storm. They spent the next few minutes rearranging a few bales of hay and fashioning a place to sit and sleep. As they did, a muddy-footed child ran in. "From ma" he said, thrusting a wrapped basket toward Thomas. Without another word, he spun on his heel and was gone. Thomas peeked lifting the cloth. Inside he found half a cold chicken, a few biscuits and a gooseberry pie. "Bless the dear lady," he said. "Supper! I was sure we were doing without!"

In a very few intense minutes the two had destroyed the chicken and biscuits and made a run at the pie. Thomas leaned back and pulled pipe and tobacco out of his haversack. He was in the midst of preparing his pipe when Jacob scolded, "Hey, she said no smoking!"

"She'll never know."

"She'll see the light or smell the smoke and we'll be out in the rain!"

"Not in this storm, Son, not in this storm." He lit his pipe and drew deeply.

Jacob shook his head in disapproval but let the matter drop. Instead he asked, "Why was that woman so rough with us?"

Thomas gave him a surprised look. "So rough? What do you mean?"

"Well, I never like seeing a gun pointed at me. And why aren't we in the house? I bet there was room."

Thomas nodded blowing out smoke. "You're right. There probably was room, but she was just protecting her own."

Jacob gave him a puzzled look, "Protecting her folks from the likes of us?"

Thomas nodded again. "Jacob, I'd wager she's all alone in that house, well 'cept for the children of course. I'd guess her husband is off with the rebels. She's alone with her brood doing her best to protect them in tough times. Strangers ride up as night falls; she has to be ready. Truthfully, I'm surprised we got any kind of shelter at all." He nudged the delivered basket with his boot, "Even a bit of supper to go along."

A fierce roll of thunder filled the barn and a very loud lightning strike shook them. It hit uncomfortably close.

"I'd guess if I'd come riding in alone, she'd have sent me on my way. Having you here might have tipped the balance in our favor."

Jacob pondered for a minute. "Didn't see it that way," he admitted. He thought a minute more. "You know, we could probably help them out by doing a few chores in the morning before we leave." He looked questioningly at Thomas.

Thomas very slowly and neatly knocked out his pipe carefully extinguishing and burying all embers. He put the pipe away. Then he looked back at Jacob. "Very interesting idea, Jacob. In fact, I'm sure that's a very good idea." He continued to look at Jacob, as if he hadn't seen him at all before.

"Can I have some more pie?"

"Sure," Thomas replied, handing over the remaining dessert.

Then he abruptly changed the subject. "Tell me Jacob, what's your impression of today?"

"What do you mean?" Jacob responded, suspicious of the change in topic.

"I'm merely asking what you thought about what you saw today. After all, you saw everything I did." Thomas sat back, waiting for an answer.

Jacob thought for a moment, trying to decide whether to give Thomas a smart-aleck answer, a real answer or no answer at all. He finally decided to respond with his own question. "Let me ask you true. Do you even know General, excuse me," he said a bit sarcastically, " I mean Lieutenant Colonel Webb?"

Thomas's answer was instantaneous, "No, I surely don't. However," he continued before Jacob could respond, "I did write to him and he responded. He truly did invite me to meet him. So it's true I stretched the truth, but I only stretched it a smite. I really did want to run into him in those camps."

Inside, Jacob smiled. He liked that answer. He'd been stretching that truth "a smite" since he'd left Salem.

Thomas pushed on. "So back to my question, what do you think about today?"

After a small pause, Jacob answered, "It's different."

Thomas jumped immediately. "What do you mean?"

"Things are not the same. The camps are different. They're more....well I suppose they're more...orderly."

"What do you base that conclusion on?"

Another pause. "Well, I spent time in camps in the District and they weren't like Camp Corcoran or Whipple. They were different."

"The camps you're familiar with were less orderly?"

Jacob nodded.

Henderson continued on, "Why do you think the camps changed? What caused it?"

This time Jacob did the appraising. He looked at Henderson, made his decision, and gave his answer. "McClellan."

"McClellan?" Henderson was surprised.

"McClellan." Jacob repeated, "I've heard the men talk."

"So you're an expert on army camps, hey? Spend a lot of time there, did you?"

Jacob jerked as if sparked, "I suppose you could say I did! At least in the Second Rhode Island and the Second Ohio camps!"

That caused Thomas to reconsider, "Well if that's true", he thought to himself "it's more than I know."

Henderson studied Jacob again and made a decision. "Jacob, my young associate, I think it's time I heard more of your story."

"Who says I want you to?" shot back Jacob instinctively.

"Your call, totally Sir, your call." Thomas said in a soothing tone, "But the lodgings, such as they are, are ours," he swept his arm around the barn space "and the night is young."

Jacob considered. Stalling for time, he took a large bite of pie. Henderson had treated him fairly so far, maybe this was in his best interest. His original plan was after all, shot to pieces. Could sharing his story somehow help him? He decided it just might, so he started.

"I was born in Indiana, southern Indiana. You know Indiana?"

"Ah, no, can't say I do."

"Well, I lived in Salem Indiana, some 40-50 miles northwest of Louisville. My pa ran a general store in Salem just like Mr. Lincoln. Did you know Mr. Lincoln once ran a store and lived in Indiana?"

"Ah, no, you've got me again. I thought he was from Illinois."

"Nah, he only moved to Illinois after he lived in Indiana. He's a southern Indiana boy just like me. Pa said he grew up about a hundred miles west of us, but I've never met him," Jacob said almost sadly. "Anyway, the four of us:, Ma, Pa, my sister, and I lived in Salem. We had a small farm but the store was the main family business." At this point, Jacob shifted around uneasily on the hay bales. He stared down at his dirty boots.

When he continued, there was a new element of sadness in his voice, a tone Thomas had not heard before. "Then a few years back, the sickness came. Not sure what it was-some kind of fever. My sister died, and it almost took away my ma. She made it through, but she was never really the same after that. Pa said she lost her sunshine. Oh, she treated us fine, but she just never got back to being the same Ma." He scuffed his boot on the barn floor. "Then this year, in the spring, the fever came back. Ma died almost as soon as it hit her, and two weeks later Pa was gone too."

Jacob looked up from the floor, but he wasn't looking at Thomas. He was back in southern Indiana, reliving the pain. "I don't really remember much about it to be truthful. They tell me I was out of my head with fever…but…at least I didn't die." Jacob continued to stare back at the past. "When I came back to the land of the living, as the parson put it, I was in town, laid up at the church. There were a few of us there, all put up in whatever they could fashion. Lots of folks were powerful sick. Some made it, some didn't. Didn't seem to be much rhyme nor reason about who lived and who died, at least not that I could see." He stopped again.

Thomas was aghast. He had never thought he would hear something like this! Jacob's life was so different from his! And to be honest, he hadn't really given much thought at all to Jacob's background. He knew after all, that Jacob appeared to be alone, and, yes, that was unusual, but that's about all the thought he had given it. He was way too wrapped up in his own thoughts and schemes to have given Jacob much thought at all. And now, to hear this terrible story.

Jacob sat silently, wrapped in the pain. Thomas didn't know what to do. Should he prompt the boy to continue? Should he attempt to comfort him? And how exactly would he even do that? Should he respect his privacy and pain and leave him be? Luckily, Jacob solved his dilemma for him by stirring, looking around a bit, and then continuing.

"Turns out Ma and Pa were both long buried by then. They needed to get folks in the ground, the townsfolk told me, and I'd been gone with the fever a good ten days or so. The parson had already found my pa's will and read it. Plans had been made and they were underway. Parson took control of my trucks and possibles. Seeing as I had no folks left in Indiana, the good folks decided the best thing would be to auction off the store and farm. I couldn't live there no more, they said, even though I was pretty sure I could." He paused again, remembering. The silence drifted on. Thomas sat, unmoving.

Finally, he could stand it no more. "What happened next, Jacob?"

"Well, it turns out, according to the will, my pa had an older sister in New York State. My Aunt Hezbalaya. Honestly, I only remember pa talking about her once, maybe twice in my whole life. Never met her. Anyway, the parson wrote to her, telling her our news and informing her that he was going to be sending me to New York to live with her. She telegraphed back and told him no. She said she didn't want to be saddled with me.

A shocked Thomas said, "She said that? She never!"

"Well, no, not in those exact words. She actually said she could not be encumbered with a young charge. Encumbered. Parson looked up the word and showed it to me in the dictionary. She made her meaning clear. She said she was an elderly spinster and could not attend a young child, but the parson wouldn't take no for an answer. He sent the proceeds of the auction to her for my security and well being. He did hold out some for me." Jacob reached inside his shirt and pulled out a small bag. He shook it so Thomas could hear the clank of a few coins. "Then the townsfolk planned out a train ride for me and got me ready to head east. No matter how much I told them I wanted to stay in Salem, they ignored me and went about their plans. Wagon ride up to Brownstown, train ride to Cincinnati, to Columbus, Pittsburgh, and eventually Washington, D.C. From there it was up to New York and Aunt Hezbayla." Jacob shook his head in sorrow.

"So how, on God's green earth did you end up here? Why aren't you in upstate New York?" Thomas was completely caught up in Jacob's story.

Jacob gave him a bit of a look and said simply, "Because I didn't want to go there."

"Oh, that was it? It was that easy?"

"I never said it was easy," Jacob instantly corrected, "I just said I didn't want to go there. Look see, my plan from the beginning was to escape that train and get back to Indiana. Maybe not Salem but someplace in Southern Indiana. That's home, after all. But there was no escape on the wagon ride up to Brownstown and the parson made darn sure I got on that train. Even talked to a conductor about me and pointed me out. So fine, I thought, I'll ride to Cincinnati. That's just across the state line from Indiana. I could make my way home alright." He ruefully shook his head, "But that plan got thwarted too. There was this woman," he filled the word woman with scorn,"who would not leave me alone. She cottoned on to me as if she were my very ma. Sitting with me, asking questions, she would not leave me alone. And of course, as it turns out, she was going to Columbus, Ohio. So I had no chance, none, to get off that train in Cincinnati. That woman stuck with me like a tick on a hound. So I was now riding from Cincinnati to Columbus."

"So you decided to make your move in Columbus then?"

"Exactly! As soon as this woman was gone, I was gone. But she got another conductor and made sure that man knew my business as well as I did. She made him promise he would take extra special care of me all the way to D.C.! I was in a spot, I'll tell you for sure."

At that Thomas had to laugh. He could just imagine how frustrated his new young friend had been by that turn of events.

"But in Pittsburgh, a beginning of an idea came aboard. I saw my first soldier. He boarded the train in Pittsburgh. I knew there was a war of course, and men from Salem had left to join, but here was a real-life soldier, in real-life uniform, heading to Washington D.C. As we made our way across Pennsylvania, an idea came to me. Maybe I could use the war to my advantage."

"You were planning on joining the army?" Thomas asked incredulously.

"Not formally join, I guess but I wondered if there might be a bit of hustle and bustle in the nation's capital and a chance for me to make my escape. And basically that's what I did! I went looking for a place to hide and found it right smack dab in the middle of the Union army! The army took over the whole capital, so I basically just joined right in the gaggle and confusion." Jacob looked up at Thomas and gave him a bit of a smile.

"Wait a minute, what did you do? You did what? I don't understand!"

"Well, Sir, here's how it went. I was supposed to transfer to a north bound train in DC so no one said boo of a word when I grabbed my possibles and left the train. But instead of getting on another train, I got off in that Union Station, and I got out the door!"

"But what happened next?" Thomas was as deep into this story as he could be. He had never heard anything quite like it and didn't exactly know what to make of it.

"Truthfully I didn't have much of a plan," Jacob admitted. "But as soon as I stepped outside, I saw man after man in uniform, swirling all around me, going every which way. The first thing I did was buy some food; the second was just to follow some soldiers around and see what was what.

At first, I just watched. Hid where I could, slept when I could, scrounged what food I could. Then after a few days, I began to see a system to the place."

"A system? What do you mean?"

"I figured out where everybody was hustling off to. Or at least a lot of people. See, there were two groups of Union soldiers in the capital then, the Second Rhode Island and the Second Ohio. So I just kinda joined in with them."

"No, no, no, wait!" Thomas protested, waving his hands at Jacob. Giving Jacob an incredulous look, he said, "Are you expecting me to believe you joined the Union Army?" He crossed his arms across his chest. "I find that remarkably hard to believe!"

"Well, no, I didn't exactly formally join; I just kind of blended in. I found a way to make a home in the camps."

"Wait, wait, wait," a protesting Thomas interrupted again. "You are a child! You were living with full-grown adults! Are you telling me no one noticed you? You must of stuck out like a sore thumb!"

"Why, what's one more youngun to a group of soldiers? They didn't have to take care of me; they ignored me. Everybody believed I belonged to someone else."

"No, that's it!" Thomas interjected again. "You're telling me a child wouldn't stand out?"

This time Jacob was giving the hard look. "I'm starting to think you never went to one of those camps. I don't believe you have any idea about what things were like!" He stared up at Thomas, accusingly. "So did ya? Did you visit either camp?"

Thomas was caught. Of course he had not visited either camp; he'd still been down in Williamsburg. "That's what I thought," Jacob snorted, clearly happy to have the upper hand. "If you had, you would have seen parcels of younguns. Lots of soldiers brought their families. There were people milling around everywhere! I was just one more body."

Thomas was incredulous. "Soldiers brought their families?"

"Sure, well, some of them did anyway, at least in the very beginning. See that's what I was trying to tell you. Back before Bull Run, things were different. It was easy come easy go. Lots of food hanging about, lots of places to grab a little sleep-eye. You didn't bother folks; they didn't bother you. They may have had some guards around, but they were usually asleep or playing cards. They certainly weren't taking guarding those camps too seriously."

Jacob paused, "Course all that changed after Bull Run. The world tightened up." He looked back up at Thomas, "You know about Bull Run?"

"That," Thomas said, " I do know about. I was there."

Jacob snorted. "You were there? Really? You were there?" He squinted at Thomas, "Or is this one of those, 'Why yes, I know General Webb.' type stories?" Thomas didn't respond to that comment.

"Hmmph." he continued, "Guess there was a chance I could'a seen you there then."

Now Thomas took on the unbelieving tone. "You're telling me you were in the battle? Say, I may believe you about the camps, but there is no way you were in the battle! I refuse to believe it!"

"I didn't say I was in the fighting, I said I was there, and I was!" He glared at Thomas daring him to challenge his statement.

Thomas stepped back. "All right, all right, tell me your tale."

"It ain't no tale," Jacob flared at him, "It's what happened!"

"Fine, fine, get on with it."

"So happens, I was sleeping those days in the Second Rhode Island Camp. The rumor started flowing around that we were due to go south, so I just figured I would go with them. Easiest thing to do."

"Then I heard their commander, Colonel Burnside," he interrupted himself, "You know him, big man, kinda funny whiskers on his face? Wears that big floppy hat? Anyway, he gave a talk to the men, getting them ready to fight. We all went back to our bivouac and the soldiers got ready to go."

"Orders came about 2:30 in the morning, (which Thomas knew from first-hand experience was true) and then we took off marching for two days. Well, that's not quite right; we didn't march for two days. We were on the road for two days. We'd march some, then stop. Then we'd march again, then stop. No one ever knew why we stopped. Sometimes men would slip away to pick berries or get water 'cause we weren't allowed breakfast or a fire. Couldn't let us sleep or even lie down, but they would keep us standing for hours. And boy was it hot! And the insects ate us up!" Jacobs hands itched his arms, reliving the bites. "It was pretty doggone disorganized, I have to tell you."

Thomas was not sure how to react to this tale. Jacob certainly had the feel and tenor of the situation. But then, he could have heard all this from any soldier's conversation. Lord knew there had been enough of those after the battle! Every man an expert!

Thomas was not convinced there was any truth in Jacob's tale, but he pushed him to continue. Maybe with enough rope he'll hang himself, Thomas thought.

"So what happened next?"

"What happened next? What happened next?" Jacob snorted with disgust, "What happened next is that I got caught."

Thomas gave him a quizzical look. "Caught?"

"Caught. We was down by Sudley Springs gettin ready to wade that crick, you know, the Bull Run? I was trailin' along and suddenly, some big hand plucked me up and this captain I'd never seen before says, 'No place for children!' and he hands me over to a corporal. That man shoved me under one arm, walked me back a pace and smacked me on the backside. 'Run home Virginia boy, before you get killed! No place for young Rebel snots here!' He pushed me away and then he was gone. I was sure going to wait for him to pass and get back toward that crick, but then, well then I heard a sound I'd never heard before. Froze my blood and scared me no end. A few seconds later a man marchin' by told me it was cannon. "Don't worry," he said, 'that cannon's a good half mile up the road.' But I decided half mile was close enough. I had absolutely no intention of getting killed, so my plans changed accordingly. I turned around and started makin' my way back up the road."

"And?" Thomas pressed.

"Then the strangest thing happened. I was makin' my way back north, against the wave of soldiers coming south when a carriage came up behind me. A man, a man in a nice suit and hat, and a pretty young lady, all dressed up, were riding on that very same road. They offered me a ride once they heard I was heading back to Washington. They said they had come down to see the rebels lose but when they had heard that cannon, well, the young lady decided she'd seen enough. So I rode home with them." Jacob paused as an idea caught him up, "You know that a ride back took us less than a day." He looked at Thomas. "It had taken us all of almost three days to get there." He shook his head.

"Well, if you were there, you know the rest. The horror, the blood, the wounded and the dead. The world changed forever that day." Jacob concluded soulfully.

"That it most certainly did." Thomas sat still, taking in all the boy had said. He was still not sure if he believed a word of the tale. It was so fantastic! Quite impossible that a boy of his age could have experienced all this! But was it so impossible? Certainly he had not experienced anything like this, but he was learning he had not experienced a lot of things. And so much of it had the ring of truth about it. "If Jacob had really done all these things," Thomas mused, "I am going to be thinking about him in a different way." After all, even tonight, in a manner, his presence had helped Thomas obtain lodging. Clearly, there were things to think about here.

"Jacob, that's quite the story. I appreciate you sharing. However, I propose an early start tomorrow, so we can get to Camp Runyon. I think we should turn in. Now," he continued before Jacob could interrupt, "I think our early start should include a pass at those chores you mentioned. That is indeed a very good idea. So, again, I suggest we tend to our bedding."

It had been a long day for Jacob as well, and he voiced no objection. The conversation ceased and the two settled in for the night falling asleep to the sounds of the rain on the barn's roof.

Chapter 4

Thomas began to blink himself awake. He slowly focused and the events of the previous day starting returning, "Hmmm, the barn." It came to him slowly. The ride, the storm, the barn. Oh, and the new companion. Jacob, was it? And then it hit him, Jacob! "Ayhh! What have I done? What was I thinking?"

Another small groan slipped out as he rolled over. He was not an old man by any means, but he felt like one this morning. Sleeping on hay piled on a dirt floor was not the same as his featherbed, smelly bedmate or not. Besides, this barn had its own share of smells.

He groaned again, continued to gather his thoughts, stretched his arms, and a bit awkwardly made his way to his feet. Jacob may have been awake or the groans may have awakened him. Either way, the boy stirred and looked up at him. Strangely enough, he had a semi-puzzled look on his face, too.

"Good morning, Jacob. Did you sleep well?" Jacob shook himself as he made it to his feet. Thomas noted that Jacob got to his feet a bit more nimbly than he had.

"Tolerably, Sir," he answered, "and you?"

"As well as can be expected, I think. Thank you." He stretched and groaned again. The image of a piping hot mug of coffee suddenly filled his mind. "Not bloody likely this morning," he said aloud earning a puzzled glance from the boy.

With that, the day began.

A quick peek out showed that the storm had moved on. The day was dawning clear, bright and blue. They quickly assembled their few things. In just a very few minutes, they were ready to be on their way. But true to his word, Thomas left the barn and walked purposely to the farmhouse. He firmly knocked on the farmhouse door.

"Good Morning, Ma'am, and a grand morning it is." Thomas said as the farmer's wife came to the door. He handed her the basket that had housed last night's supper. "We'd like to thank you for the night's shelter and for the supper. As you can see," he turned waving an arm back toward the barn, "everything is as it was. Bristol shape! To thank you for your hospitality, my assistant and I would like to do a few chores, to help the family out."

His assistant? Jacob scrunched his face and gave Thomas a look. Assistant? What was this about?

The farmwife was hesitant, but after a few seconds, gave in accepting the help. She pointed them toward a few tasks and the two went to work. Thomas was a bit surprised to find that he and Jacob fell into an easy working rhythm. The chores were quickly and efficiently done. Thomas returned to the door. "There you are my good lady. And thank you again for the shelter and food. We most sincerely appreciate it."

The woman, obviously a bit surprised by the quality and speed of the work, said a single word, "Wait". She turned away from the door. Returning a short minute later, she surprised them by thrusting a wrapped bundle in Jacob's arms. "A bit of breakfast, to start you on your journey." she said, in a half embarrassed voice. Then she turned away quickly closing the door.

"Now that's a pleasant surprise." said Thomas appreciatively as they walked toward the horse. They mounted and rode out of the farmyard. "On to Camp Runyon." Thomas announced rather grandly.

As they rode, Thomas gave thought to his, well, no to be fair, their situation. Now that he was awake and in the full glow of the day, he realized it was time to do some considering. He was in some kind of a situation here. It was true that he had gone off half-cocked agreeing to take Jacob to St. Anne's. But it was equally true that taking Jacob from the good sergeant probably was a smart move in terms of cultivating a news source. And having Jacob around last night had probably guaranteed their housing. And when Thomas thought about the life journey Jacob had experienced, well, it was nothing like anything Thomas had been forced to experience. Thomas' big battle was avoiding college in New York? Jacob had seen his family die. And then he had been forced to make his own way in the middle of a war! He had to admit, Jacob's story, if true of course, was quite impressive. Jacob had gone through tough times, and he was resourceful enough to pull off a journey that gave Thomas pause. But still, what did Thomas really know about the boy? It was only one day after all. Thoughts continued to roil.

They hadn't gone too far though before the promise of breakfast pulled at Thomas. "I'm in favor of breakfast. You?" he asked. Jacob quickly agreed and Thomas stopped under a large oak tree. Jacob jumped down and Thomas tied the horse. He unwrapped the bundle, finding cucumbers, a bit of cabbage, some huckleberries, and a generous piece of cornmeal.

"It may not look like much," Thomas commented, "but it was kind of her to share. I'm sure they don't have extra."

"Looks fine to me!" Jacob quickly countered. "And I'm happy to have it. I've made do with far worse." His stomach rumbled as if to prove his point.

They sat in the shade of the tree. The sun was well up; the day was proving to be warm and clear. The war seemed far away. The two sat quietly, enjoying the meal.

When they finished, Thomas gestured toward a nearby creek, "Shall we fill the canteens for the trip?"

Jacob untied them from the pack, and they started toward the water.

Abruptly, Thomas made another decision. He hoped, he was not once again, going off half-cocked.

"You know, Jacob, I've been thinking a bit about your situation."

"Hmm?" said Jacob continuing toward the creek. He had found that a noncommittal answer worked well much of the time.

"After hearing your tale, I am sure you do not want to go to New York and live with your spinster aunt."

"Hmm," murmured Jacob again, not willing to agree to anything. After all, he had no idea where this was going. He uncapped the canteens.

"And neither of us know anything about St. Anne's, It might be a great situation, it may not be.'

"Hmm-hmm," Jacob was sure it was not the thing for him, but it didn't seem the time to announce that. He plunged the canteens into the creek.

"So I have a proposition for you." Thomas said. He was amazed to find himself saying this, but he had to admit, it felt right. "Just think on this - what would you think about working for me, you know like an assistant, or apprentice?"

Now that got Jacob's attention. He took his time turning slowly back to Thomas. There was that word again, "assistant." "I'm not sure I fully understand."

"Well, to be honest, I'm not sure I fully understand either." Thomas paused and looked around at nothing. He took an idle step toward the creek. "This is new territory for me, Jacob, I can promise you."

"Let me share my thoughts with you please, Jacob, and then I'll be happy to hear your reaction." He took a deep breath. "You are a young man of some obvious talents. I think you're passable smart; you're quick on your feet; you're obviously enterprising. For proof of that, just look at how you've lived since Salem."

Jacob merely nodded, looking straight into Thomas's eyes.

"I believe you can help me. You can help me with research. You can go places, why you can go places I can't and probably hear things I wouldn't hear. You could be a valuable asset. " Jacob made no sound but continued to stare fixedly at him. A bit unnerved at the stony reaction, Thomas' next words came out in a rush. "And equally, I believe I can help you. I believe we could form a sort of partnership that would suit us both."

"Jacob, I think I am on the edge of a big story, here, a very big story. Maybe even a huge story. This is no longer the army that got beat at Bull Run. It's changed. It's more confident, more trained, more professional. And it's not just one camp, I see it all around. That story needs to be shared with the Country!"

Jacob heard the capital "C" in Thomas's words but sat quietly. Then after a moment's pause, he asked, "And you believe you're the one to share it with them?" His tone was skeptical.

"Yes," Thomas answered. He took another deep breath. "Perhaps, with your help. This is a big story, and I intend to commit to it. I want to write this. Look around, this is a new war; it's a new army, new spirit; they even have a new name…" He paused, suddenly drawing a blank.

"Army of the Potomac," Jacob dryly offered.

Thomas jumped. "Yes, yes, exactly. See you hear things! We'd be a great team.", getting more excited as he talked. He paused again, taking the time to frame his argument. "Jacob, I feel as if I am at the foot of a great stairway. That stairway leads up and I think we are meant to climb it!"

"We!?!?" Jacob asked. "We? We've just met!" He was stalling for time. But as he spoke, he thought. "Well, he certainly has a way with words. Perhaps he can write as well."

He decided to go down a different road. Changing tack he asked, "So this would be a paying job?"

"Absolutely!" Thomas instantly responded, "A dime a day. Shall we say six days a week?" He looked hard at Jacob searching for a response. He plunged on. "In addition, I'll provide room and two meals a day." He again held up a hand of warning, "Though, let me be clear. I can't promise the food will be fancy. You'll sleep where I do, eat what I eat. I think the last twenty four hours may be a fair indicator."

He looked Jacob full in the face. "So what do you think, Jacob? Is this a better chance than St. Annes?"

Now, it was Jacob's turn to do some thinking. He had known this man for less than two days. He seemed fair enough, so far, but hard experience had taught Jacob that initial impressions could mean little. Jacob was certainly not ready to tie his horse to this man's wagon. Of course, it did bear thinking. He did not want to go to his aunts and this offer got him out of that. He did not want to go to St. Anne's. But his next question was: where would it be easier? Escape from St. Anne's or from this man?

He continued to weigh his options. He knew Thomas did not always tell the truth, but he had been square with him so far. They had found a roof and food, all of which was very important to Jacob. Jacob also had seen the difference in the army since Bull Run. He hadn't really organized it in his mind truth be told, but when Thomas put it like that, he realized the man was right. There may well be a story there. He did not know however if Henderson was the man to tell it.

The main thing he kept coming back to, in the few minutes he'd had to ponder the question, was escape. Most importantly, it seemed like he would be able to escape whenever he wanted from this man. Why he could have bolted last night and Thomas would have been none the wiser! A little voice in his head said, "Perhaps better the devil you know than the one you don't, hey Jacob? At least for the short term."

And that, in the end, made the difference.

"So tell me more, what exactly would I be doing?"

Thomas was ready for that question. "I aim to be the best reporter in Virginia, or wherever else this war takes me. To do that, I need information, I need research. You'll help me get that. I'll point you places, but I am also going to count on you to keep your eyes and ears open as you go around. You already do that. You get that information and you share it with me. You're creative. Why if half of that tale you told me yesterday is true…"

Jacob erupted, "Half! Half!" he sputtered "Every single God given word was the truth, the Lord's very truth! If you don't believe that, I guess we'll end this right here!"

Taking a half step backward, Thomas waved a hand in surrender.

"Forgive me, forgive me. It's all true, I accept it all."

Jacob allowed that to calm him down a bit. "Okay let's go over this one more time. You're offering me a job, 10 cents a day, six days a week. I'll do research for you and help you gather information about this story. I get a roof over my head and a bed. I get two meals a day. Is that about it?"

Thomas nodded. "Yes, though we may be on the road some, like now" he said gesturing around, "So I can't guarantee that roof part. When we're in the city you'll be helping me, except of course for that half day every week you spend in school."

'School!" Jacob sputtered, "you never said nothin' about no school! School!" he spat again. "I've done school. I'm finished with school." In a lower voice, he repeated even more firmly "I'm finished with school!"

Thomas looked at him, with a satisfied but somewhat ironic smile on his face.

"I would counter the grammar in that sentence proves otherwise, but fair is fair. Answer me these three questions and we'll discuss it." Thomas held up three fingers, "Who's the third president of the United States, what's the largest state in the country, based on land size east of the Mississippi and what is 12+10+12?"

The three fingers remained in the air as he waited for Jacob to answer. Jacob glared resentfully at Thomas and after a few seconds answered. "Thomas Jefferson was the third president, my pa taught me. The largest in which country? Union or Confederate, you didn't say." Another pause and he ended with a bit of regret, "And I'd need a ciphering board to answer the last."

Thomas nodded. "One - Jefferson is correct. Two - don't be a smart alec, the Union is our country, and Georgia is the largest state east of the Mississippi. Three, 12+10+12 is 34."

"Well, say what you mean then!" Jacob shot at him, attempting to get the board tipped back in his favor. "I can't read your mind to see what country you mean!" He almost added that Georgia wasn't currently in the country, but thought better of it.

Thomas shook his head at the boy, " Listen Jacob, as you heard, I went to college. I can promise you the more you know, the farther you will go in this world. More importantly for me, the more you know, the more you can help me. The more you help me, the more value you have; the more value you have, the more you earn. Makes sense, yes?"

Jacob did not like the sound of school one bit! Attending school was most certainly not in his plan. But the trouble was he had almost already decided to accept Thomas' offer. It kept him out of New York and out of Saint Anne's. He didn't know anything about Saint Annes but he had to guess it would more strict than life with Thomas. And Thomas he guessed, was the easier one to escape from. But school!

Then Jacob brightened as a thought hit him. When he escaped, this school nonsense would not matter a whit! And if Thomas was already talking about increasing his pay, so much the better. He'd take whatever pay he could get before he went his own way, so he could agree to anything now! A little voice in his head advised him, "Say yes and be done with it!" A load lifted and he offered his handshake to Thomas.

"Mr. Henderson," he said to Thomas, "I accept."

Thomas grabbed the offered hand and shook. "Right! Well then Mr. Assistant, let's get to work!"

The practical voice in Thomas' head said, "Uh-oh, you've stepped in it now! " But Thomas merely shook his head and said softly, "Maybe, maybe not." He had a feeling about this newly-founded partnership.

Chapter 5

After coming to their arrangement, the two rode on to Camp Runyon. It was much like the other camps they had visited. As they left the camp, Thomas was even more sure he was on the right path. He had the beginnings of a story, but he needed a lot more information. "Now, how exactly can I get that information?" he excitedly asked Jacob. Clearly it was time to lay out a course of action. The first step in the action plan was to return to the capital. The second step was to obtain an accurate map of the Washington, D.C. area.

They poured over the map carefully noting the location of all the newly-built forts. Together they then worked out a plan. After that, it was time to hit the road.

Over the next few weeks, they visited all the camps they could. Camps Whipple, Corcoran, Washington, Richardson - all were visited. Some were in Maryland, some were in Virginia. At some camps, they were welcomed. At others they were met with stony stares, loaded guns, and insinuations that they were probably Secesh spies.

They put in the miles. And Thomas kept his promise about food and lodging. Wherever he slept, Jacob slept. Occasionally they would sleep in a tavern. Sometimes, as they had the first night, in a barn. Sometimes under the stars. Once those stars gave way to thunderstorms, and they were soaked. Not much sleep that night, but they were both equally soaked. When day broke, they got up and headed on their way.

Whatever Thomas ate, Jacob ate as well. Sometimes they ate well, sometimes, well, a person can always do without food, for a little while. A very little while according to Jacob.

But no matter the weather or road conditions, the two traveled taking notes and trying to figure out what was going on with this army.

There were times when Thomas could clearly see that it really helped to have Jacob by his side. The presence of a younger person seemed to soften many guards' worries. Occasionally if the two were welcomed and allowed in, they were even offered the chance to share the soldiers' meals. They ate pork, beans and hominy, and they listened. And they learned.

Later, when they sat alone by a campfire or at a quiet table together, they compared notes. They both agreed that there truly was a story here. Not only had this army changed; it was continuing to change. A captain from New York that Thomas happened upon said it best, "Listen, you've got to understand! Before Little Mac..."

"Wait, Little Mac?" Thomas interrupted. They were sitting in a Washington, D.C. tavern. They were in the tavern because Thomas had promised to buy the drinks. The coins were flying from his purse, but he felt he was so close to something big that he put his rapidly decreasing bank account out of his mind. "I'll worry about that tomorrow", he promised himself.

"Yes, Little Mac." the captain continued. "That's what the men have named him. They love him. He rides through the camp and the men erupt in cheers. They toss their hats; they chant his name. They love him, and they know he loves them."

"Wait," Thomas interrupted again. "But I thought he was whipping them into shape. Doesn't he make them work? Doesn't he make them sweat? They love a man who puts them through that?"

"Indeed he does make them work, make them sweat," the captain heartedly agreed. "In fact, that's why they love him."

"Hmm, missing something here," Thomas said, almost to himself.

"Look, you don't understand. Before Little Mac came, the army was a mess. Hell, it wasn't even an army, it was a gang of untrained men all living together with too much time on their hands and too little discipline. The capital was a mess; the war was a mess. Little Mac fixed that. Soldiers like that, they appreciate that."

The captain leaned closer to Thomas as he drove his point home.

"You've got to remember, deep down, most soldiers like order. We may not admit it, but we prefer order. Before Mac came undisciplined soldiers were everywhere. Men who should have been in their camps, well, they filled the taverns every night. They peacocked about! They were wallpapered! Men wandered drunkingly from one saloon to the next until they were too drunk to get back to camp. It was terrible. No one seemed to be in charge; no one seemed to care.

And then Little Mac got here. He took a look at things and suddenly there were changes-big changes! Soldiers were warned that the taverns were off limits and then trustworthy soldiers were assigned to police the mess. Suddenly the taverns and saloons were being patrolled nightly. If you were out on the street or in a tavern, you'd better have a pass; you'd better be able to state your business straightaway. That tidied things up right quick-like, it did. Mac restored order."

The captain paused to take a long draw from his mug. "Ahh," he said, wiping his mouth. He twisted toward the bar, got the bartender's attention, and signaled for a refill. Then he turned his attention back to Thomas.

"But he did more. He didn't stop there! He turned those cesspools we called camps into military organizations. He reorganized them and got them cleaned up. He got those camps cleaned up; he got those soldiers cleaned up. He made sure the men got meals, good meals. He drilled them and drilled them and drilled them. Then after we drilled, he put us on parade. Slowly, we began to see ourselves as soldiers. Shoot, we became soldiers. We weren't the untrained mob that went to Bull Run anymore. We became the Army of the Potomac!" He banged his tankard on the table for emphasis. "We're an army, by God!" Thomas nodded his understanding and he wrote it all down.

After that meeting, Thomas was ready to start writing. For the time being, he was finished with his tour of the forts and the taverns. Two days later, he emerged with several pages filled with his impressions about the newly formed Army of the Potomac. Jacob was impressed and told Thomas so. "I'm glad you're impressed.' he said. "You played a big role in getting this story together." Then Thomas put his hat on and folded the papers under his arm. "Now it's time to see if Mr. Comstock is equally impressed!" And he headed off to the telegraph office.

Three days later, Thomas came running into the room. "Jacob!" he shouted. "Jacob!!" He was waving a telegraph in his hand.

Jacob looked up, giving Thomas the "Well what?" look.

"We've done it! We're published!!" Thomas did a small celebratory dance as he pushed the telegraph toward Jacob. "He loved it. Called it my best work yet!" Not that that was so impressive considering how much he'd had published, but it was a nice comment never-the-less.

"He says, and I quote, 'outstanding work. Stop. Too much for one story. Stop. Will run Monday, Tuesday and Wednesday, next. Stop. Agreed upon payment will be forthcoming. Stop. Suggestions for more stories will follow. Stop.' "

An equally big smile grew on Jacob's face. He stood and extended his hand, "Congratulations, Mr. Henderson, you are a published reporter. I can't wait to read it."

And as it turned out of course, Jacob wasn't the only one to read it. A week after the first article ran under the byline, "By Thomas Henderson, war correspondent," Thomas received a letter from New York. It was an editor of a competing paper asking Thomas if he were interested in changing jobs. The next day brought a letter from his father. His father had been shown the article and was very impressed. He praised his son for his work and his contribution to the war. "You're helping people up here understand what is really going on with that army." he wrote. They understood, of course, that for the time period, continuing college was out of the question. Thomas could not continue his studies in a foreign country or in a war zone, so they had decided to extend a monthly stipend to Thomas. "Just until the war ended and he could get back to his medical studies". Until then, they applauded him for his good work. He did say that they were worried about him being so close to the fighting, but they were glad he was not in the army. His father concluded by saying he believed nothing was worse than a civil war.

The beginning of tears in his eyes, Thomas looked at Jacob, "And I was sure he would be against this venture." He shook his head, "I don't think I will ever fully figure my parents out."

Thomas and Jacob also received another bit of good news when another note arrived. Upon his first arrival in town, Thomas had approached the Dodge House, a rooming house downtown, asking for a room. Like everywhere else, the Dodge House was full. Would he like to put his name on a waiting list? He had and had also periodically checked back with the manager. Waiting apparently paid off as the note was from the manager of the Dodge House. He had a room coming available. Did Thomas want it? Honestly, Thomas currently did not have the money to make such a move, but he immediately accepted the offer. Anything to get out of the barn!

With Jacob's help, they bid goodbye to Georgetown and gratefully set up housekeeping in the Dodge House. It was a wonderful location, on D Street, near 1st St. NW. From the one window in the room, they could see the dome that was being added to the U.S capitol building.

A third letter arrived. This one was from his publisher. It contained his pay and Mr. Alpheus R. Comstock outlined three more articles he suggested Thomas pursue. Thomas was thrilled.

The following days brought more letters and telegrams, all forwarded from his newspaper. People he had not heard from in years saw his name in the paper and reached out. Old classmates, neighbors, even some folks he did not even remember. "Getting your name splashed across a New York newspaper a few days in a row seems to get you noticed," Thomas commented. His ego swelled, but little else changed. Until he got the special letter. Then, things dramatically changed.

It started as a normal work day. Thomas and Jacob spent the day beating the streets, searching for information for a new story. By the time they got back to the Dodge House, it was dinnertime, and they were both footsore, tired, and hungry. Dinner was the most pressing thing on their minds. All thoughts of food vanished, however, when Thomas unlocked the door. A single envelope lay waiting for him just inside the room.

"Jacob," he whispered. It was addressed to "Mr. Thomas Henderson, c/o the Dodge House, Washington, D.C." The return address simply read "War Department, Washington, D.C."

"The War Department!" Jacob's eyes widened. He paused the smallest of seconds before asking, "Now what trouble are you in?"

"Me?!" Thomas said, "I might ask the same of you."

Thomas picked the letter up and studied it.

Jacob, impatient as ever, hissed, "Aren't you going to open it?"
Thomas slightly shook himself, then slit the letter open. He read silently.

After a very few seconds, a very few, Jacob demanded, "Well?"

As if he could not believe it, Thomas said, "Lieutenant Colonel Webb has invited me to the War Department for a visit this Friday. He asks if it's convenient! Jacob, how quickly can you take a message to the War Department?"

"How long is it gonna take you to write it?" Jacob countered.

Message in hand, Jacob took off for the relatively short trip to the War Department. Thomas began pacing the room. "This could be the beginning of everything," he told himself. Then thirty seconds later, "But don't get in front of yourself;
it could be a simple social invite, Nothing to it." Two more trips around the room, "But why would he invite me for a

social call? The man doesn't know me. It's got to mean something." Another wall to wall trip, "But he is from New York; perhaps it's just because he saw a New York writer here in D.C. And I did write him…"

The monologue was interrupted in mid-rant as Thomas was suddenly hit with a disturbing thought. They'd been riding all over the summer countryside; dust, dirt, rain, mud, all part of the trip. At the beginning of the research trip, his clothes had been in decent shape (or perhaps just decent enough for a college student), but they had since been frazzled by the long miles and hours. They certainly were not the clothes of a professional writer. They were not the clothes a reporter needed to meet an important person at the War Department either. "I need a new set of clothes!" he moaned with a sinking feeling. "How in the world can that be done by Friday?" The wall-to-wall marching resumed. "Perhaps the Gentleman's Emporium will have something." he thought. "And thank goodness I just got paid!"

Then the second thought hit him. If he hoped to use Jacob as an assistant, and if Jacob were going to get into the places Thomas hoped to send him, Jacob would need new clothes as well. Well, perhaps just some new clothes. Those pennies were again flowing out of his purse at an alarming rate. Thomas began to see this as a disturbing pattern.

Suddenly Thomas became aware that quite a few minutes had passed since Jacob had run out into the evening. Thomas wasn't exactly worried, but he was beginning to wonder.

It turned out Jacob had good reason for his tardiness. As luck would have it, Lieutenant Colonel Webb had been in and had written a reply on the spot. They had an appointment.

"That settles it!" Thomas excitedly said. "It's time to go clothes shopping! Let's go." He started to gather his things. Jacob had other ideas.

"Hold on right there!" Jacob vehemently protested. " I hope you're not including me in that errand! I've got perfectly fine clothes. You're not getting me all dolled up! Not going to happen! I don't need no new clothes! Besides, I want dinner! " He folded his arms defiantly across his chest and glared at Thomas. "I'm hungry!"

"Fine," Thomas agreed remembering the time. "First thing tomorrow!"

"Hmmph," Jacob snorted, then in a quiet voice he said, "We'll see about that."

"We will indeed," Thomas answered firmly.

True to his word, as soon as the next day's breakfast had been consumed, Thomas turned to Jacob. "Please follow me." He walked toward the door, obviously fully expecting Jacob to follow.

"I am not going to some tailors!" Jacob called at Thomas's back.

Thomas, continuing to walk, gave a half turn back toward the boy. "Fine, no tailors for now." he said, waving a dismissing hand. Thomas continued out the door.

After a minute's hesitation, Jacob rumbled down the stairs after him. He caught him at the ground floor, and the two exited the building. Without a word they walked east down D Street, then took a left turn on 1st, heading south.

A very few minutes later, Thomas led Jacob to an empty bench on the grounds of the United States Capitol. Thomas gave Jacob a moment to look around, and then pointed at the Capitol. "And that Jacob, is where the nation's laws are created."

A instant response. "I know that!" It was delivered in a tone Thomas was getting very used to. The tone was the one that proclaimed 'I"m not an idiot, you know.'

Thomas pointed to one side of the gleaming white building and then to the other. "There sits the Senate and there the House of Representatives."

This statement puzzled Jacob. His question slipped out before he could consider how it might make him look. "But I thought Congress sat there. Where's Congress?"

Instead of answering, Thomas poised a question of his own. "Jacob, I have to ask you." He turned to look Jacob fully in the face. "Over the last few weeks you have had plenty of chances to disappear. Why haven't you? Wasn't that part of your master plan? Why are you still here?"

The question caught Jacob unawares. His mouth fell slightly open. He was not ready with an answer. He truly had not expected the question.

It was a question he had asked himself but not fully answered. Now he was on the spot.

"Well, uhmm," he kicked a rock with his boot toe rubbing the toe around in the dirt. "I guess, it's because… well.." He squirmed on the bench. How could he give

Thomas an answer when he hadn't satisfactorily answered that question himself?

"I just haven't, that's all!" he finally muttered.

Thomas nodded as if understanding. "Let me put it another way. Are you happy with your current situation?"

"Happy?" he responded, stalling for time. "Well, sure, I mean I guess, pretty much so…"

Thomas waved his hand as if to push away a bothersome fly. "Let me start again. When I first asked you to accompany me, I was in one set of circumstances. I think you'd agree things have changed since then. Given that change, I think it's only fair to let you reassess your answer. I think I'm moving in a different game now Jacob. So I need to ask you, do you think you want to move in that game? Do you want to be a part of it?"

Jacob stalled for time. "I'm not sure I know exactly what you're asking."

Thomas nodded and sat thinking for a minute.

"Look at us now," Thomas began. "In two days we'll be meeting with people in the War Department. Important people! These new stories we're pursuing, well, they're going to take us all over town. Why, they may well take us right up to and through the doors of this very building." he said, pointing at the capital.

Thomas looked at Jacob again gauging his interest. "We need to be asking people, possibly important people, questions." His voice rose and he spoke with a bit of fervor. "We need to be getting information and writing stories about what's going on. We have important business to conduct! So I ask you again, do you want to be part of this? Do you want in the game?"

From his tone alone, Jacob knew Thomas was very serious. After a minute he said, "Yes, Sir, I believe I do."

Thomas looked hard at Jacob, staring as if were trying to read Jacob's thoughts. A few more seconds of intense staring passed and then he nodded.

"Then there's work to be done." Thomas said quietly. Then he plunged right on. "Now the thing is, you and I, we're visitors to this new world. These folks live here! It's their world!" He waved at the men heading in and out of the Capitol building. "We're on their turf; we need to ask them questions and favors. Frankly, we need to fit in. We need to be accepted."

Jacob nodded his understanding though he was not exactly sure what this was all about.

"If they take one look at us or hear one word that makes it obvious we aren't part of their world, they just may ignore us. Do you understand that?"

Jacob did understand. He had been ignored by many people.

"So that is why, if we want to stay in this new set of circumstances, we, both of us, need to make a few changes, important changes. Now you may not want to make those changes, but if you want to stay, I'm afraid you'll have to."

He paused to let his words sink in, and Jacob in return, let them sink in. He took the chance to think again about his situation. It was true he had not made any attempt to run away. It was true that he could leave whenever he chose. Why he could have just kept going

when he left for the War Department last evening! But then
there was that question again, "Where would he go? What
would he do? How would he eat?" He really did not see a
future in hiding in army camps any longer. And then there
was the fact that he liked Thomas. He found he liked the
work they were doing and heck, it was exciting, in its way.
Heck, it might even turn out to be important. He liked
Washington, D.C. True it wasn't Salem, but he liked it. He
had a roof, most nights, and food almost every day. If he
thought about it, he was in a far better place than he had
had any hope of reaching. Sitting on that wagon with
Sergeant Emerson seemed like a long, long time ago. But
still? What exactly was Thomas asking?

He looked up. "I think I understand, mostly but
what exactly are you saying?"

Thomas nodded again. "Let me spell it out. We
both need to clean up our act a bit. We need new clothes, at
least some, if we're to walk the walls and halls of
Washington." He held up a hand before Jacob could
interrupt. "Your clothes were fine for the farm and store of
Salem, Indiana and mine might have been fine for the halls
of William and Mary, but we're not in those places
anymore. We need to fit in here, not there."

Jacob didn't like to admit that, but he realized it
was true. As a ragamuffin child, staying in his "father's"
army camp, his clothes had drawn no attention. In fact
they made it easy to blend in. But to walk into the War
Department and ask for Lieutenant Colonels, well. Jacob
took Thomas' point.

"And that" said Thomas, pointing to the Capitol, "is the reason you have to go for lessons half a day each week."

"What the Congress?"

"No, the fact you didn't know there was a House and a Senate. Uh-uh," he said looking at Jacob's reaction. "You'd thought I'd forgotten but I haven't. You need to learn more about this game if you are going to play it successfully."

"Look Jacob, you're a smart young man. I know that; it's obvious. No one but a smart lad could have designed and then finagled the trip you took to get here. You lived on your own. But again, what was fine knowledge for Salem, Indiana, no disrespect to Salem, is not going to cut it in Washington, D.C. in 1861!"

Again the question slipped out, almost before Jacob could stop it. "Well okay then! There's two Congresses! Why do they have to have two and who are the people from Indiana in there?"

Thomas laughed. "Fine, I'll answer both questions, second one first. I don't know who is from Indiana..."

"Well there you are then, Mr. Smarty Pants college man from New York," Jacob interrupted. "You don't know either!"

"Ah yes, no educated, or uneducated man for that matter, knows it all. But," again he raised his hand to stop the onslaught, "an educated man knows how to find out. And I will. I also know the answer to the first question, but it takes a bit longer than I want to spend on the subject now. Instead of talking, let me show you something. I think it will help make my point about the need for education." He looked at Jacob and said, "Plus, I hope you enjoy it."

Jacob stood up. "Where to?"

"We are off to the Smithsonian."

"To the Castle?"

"The very place! Have you ever been?"

"No, Sir," came the reply. Thomas noticed a bit of interest in Jacob's voice.

A few short minutes later, they were on B street, heading toward the front door of what was known to many D.C. residents as The Castle.

By the end of the day, Jacob readily admitted he had never seen the like. Even the experienced New Yorker saw some sights during their visit.

They visited the Apparatus Room containing electrical machines Jacob had not even dreamt of. They walked past the 20-foot-tall Great Barometer. They saw over 100 portraits of Native Americans, and this was all on the first floor. A trip up stairs showed them displays of animals, minerals, fossils and even a piece of a meteorite.

As they exited the building Thomas said "Understanding all this, Jacob, is the reason to get an education." Jacob could only nod his agreement; he was too overwhelmed to do more.

If they were overwhelmed on Wednesday, their worlds turned upside down two days later. On Friday afternoon, they made their way down 17th Street towards the US War Department. On the way, Jacob said, "I know you said you've never met Lieutenant Colonel Webb. What do you know about him?"

"Basically only what I've heard from my father and around town in New York. He's from a very prominent New York family, a military family. I think his grandfather served with George Washington, but I could be wrong about that. Our family knows their family, as these things sometimes happen. I know the Lieutenant Colonel went to West Point, and I know he was at Bull Run. I didn't see him that day, but I know he was there. I primarily wrote him out of the blue, hoping to lean on our New York connection.""I'm very glad he answered our letter but truthfully I was a little surprised. I never expected an invitation to visit. And yet, here we go. The world does move in strange ways, Jacob."

When they arrived at the War Department, they presented their credentials to the corporal on duty. They were asked to wait. After a few minutes, a lieutenant came down the stairway. "Mr. Henderson? I'm Lieutenant Smithson. Lieutenant Colonel Webb asked me to bring you up. If you'll both come this way please." He gestured toward the top of the stairs and then started energetically making his way back up the stairs.

Thomas was a little surprised that Jacob was included in the invitation but he didn't say anything. Instead they both jumped to follow the quickly moving lieutenant. Topping the stairs, they turned down a hallway before coming to an abrupt halt outside a large wooden door. Lieutenant Smithson rapped sharply once and turned the knob. He motioned the two inside. As they entered he announced, "Your visitors, Lieutenant Colonel Webb."

A large well built dark haired man with a full goatee, rose from his desk. He strode across the room, extending a hand as he walked. "Mr. Henderson! At last we meet." He shook Thomas' hand enthusiastically. "It is a true pleasure, Sir."

Thomas gave the lieutenant colonel a small bow. "The pleasure is all mine, Sir. Thank you so much for taking the time."

Webb turned his attention to Jacob. "And who might this be?" he asked, offering his hand to Jacob.

"This is my assistant, Jacob Bunten, recently of Indiana."

"Indiana, heh? Fine country, I hear. Pleasure to meet you as well, Jacob."

Jacob, more than a bit tongue tied, stuttered out "My..uh…my pleasure, Sir."

Webb turned his attention back to Henderson. "I have to tell you, Mr. Henderson, your article made quite the little splash around here."

Thomas looked at him blankly for a minute. "My article? I mean you read the article? My article?"

Webb gave a small laugh at Thomas' apparent astonishment. "Your articles! All three of them. We actually read quite a few newspapers around here. It's a good way to get a feel for the nation's pulse, you know."

Thomas opened his mouth to agree when the large wooden door was thrown open.

"Webb! Webb! Where is he? Where's that reporter?"

Both Thomas and Jacob were truly shocked as they turned toward the voice and saw General George Briton McClellan. Though the general was not a large man, he seemed to fill the room.

"So this is the man, Webb?" Without waiting for an answer he offered his hand to the flabbergasted reporter. "This is the famous New York reporter, Thomas Henderson?" Little Mac didn't give anyone a chance to respond to his questions. "Nice to meet you, Sir, nice to meet you. I enjoyed the articles. Well written, good for the country to read!"

This time it was Thomas' turn to stutter. "Thank you Sir." he managed.

Then, as quickly as that, it was over. General McClellan spun on his heel. As he breezed out of the room, he called back over his shoulder, "Keep up the good work, Sir. Your nation needs men like you in this time of peril!" The door clicked close and the General was gone.

For a second, Thomas had the odd feeling that the general had taken all the air in the room with him when he left. "What just happened?" he asked in a small voice.

Webb laughed. "And that my dear Misters Henderson and Bunten was General McClellan. As you can tell, he also reads the papers. And you can also tell, he is a man of great energy. He never stops. He keeps an eye on everything, he is the master organizer, the master motivator, the man in charge. He saw your article, read it and was impressed. Your article helped the Army of the Potomac. For that, the general just gave you his thanks."

Thomas and Jacob stood flummoxed. Jacob silently took stock. They were standing in the War Department by special invitation, they had met Lieutenant Colonel Webb and now they had just met General McClellan! By golly what a day!

And that was just the first of many good days for Thomas and Jacob. The two were over the moon. After that handshake with the General, things to magically improve. Thomas was granted more and more access to the Army of the Potomac. He visited the camps, talked to the men, and joined officers for evenings at the Willard Hotel. One night at Willard's, he heard a colonel quote General McClellan, "I heard him say as clear as day, 'I flatter myself that Beauregard has gained his last victory." That quote got Thomas a headline above the fold, as they say in journalism.

On one return visit to Lieutenant Colonel Webb's office, he was introduced to a medical man, Doctor Jonathan Letterman of Pennsylvania. Doctor Letterman was a graduate of the Jefferson Medical College. As luck would have it, Doctor Letterman had once met Thomas's father and he professed himself equally happy to make Thomas' acquaintance. It was a fortunate connection for Thomas and another good source of information.

All that led to more and more stories, good stories. It turned out Thomas' time was William and Mary was not wasted, (well not all of it.) Thomas could write a good story, just as he had promised Jacob. Thomas was becoming known. His byline appeared on his stories and he as building a reputation as a fair, thorough reporter. That in turn brought more access, and more "talks" with "the men who counted" in Washington.

Mr. Comstock welcomed the stories and welcomed the increased circulation of the New York *Constitutionalist*. After the fourth above the fold article, Thomas opened his mail to find a nice letter and an even nicer promise of a pay raise. It seemed Mr. Comstock did not want to lose Thomas to a New York paper, or any paper for that matter. Thomas wondered if Mr. Comstock might have heard about his job offer from the other New York paper.

Mr. Comstock kept his promise and Thomas began receiving larger checks. Thomas and Jacob began eating a little better. Never one to complain about free food, Jacob nonetheless appreciated the improved fare. There was a bit more food and Jacob believed it was tastier. Larger quantities of tasty food was never a bad deal in his book.

They changed rooms at the Dodge House. With the new pay, Thomas could afford a larger suite of rooms. Jacob approved of the increased space, but he could see little use for the washtub and pitcher that came with the suite. Thomas began stopping by his tailor a bit more frequently. New clothes began to appear in his armoire.

Few new clothes appeared for Jacob, which was just fine with him but his life was improving in other ways as well. He liked the work, he enjoyed the bit of prestige that came with it. He enjoyed delivering Thomas' messages and waiting for replies. He enjoyed walking "the Halls of Congress."

He also had to admit that his previous education was not adequate for his current job (though he would never admit that to Thomas of course.) So he worked on his reading and writing. He worked on his spelling and composition. He only complained when he was sure Thomas was listening. "Why are there so many silly rules? Why does I come after E except after C? Why is it unacceptable to end a sentence with a preposition? And who in the world cares anyway?"

But Jacob worked on understanding the rules. He was secretly proud that he even knew what a preposition was. What used to be "Where's it at?" became "Where is it?" or sometimes even, "Where might it be?". With all respect to the letter R, he learned it did not live in the word "wash". He no longer "warshed his body" and he now knew the first president's name was Washington, not "WaRRshington". And that little body of water that flowed back on the farm was a creek, not a crik. He complained to Thomas, but Jacob really was pleased with his improvement.

Thomas was pleased as well. The improvement was easy to see. Thomas handed Jacob more responsibility and more pay. Jacob was often sent to important people with Thomas' requests for information. Jacob had seen so many officers that anyone with a rank lower than colonel got no more attention from him than the doormen at Willard's.

All of this crystalized for Jacob one day as he sat in a senator's outer office patiently waiting for a reply. He suddenly realized he had not even thought of leaving

Thomas for…days now? Weeks? He also realized he had no interest in leaving Thomas. He missed his family terribly, but he knew they were gone. There was nothing for him back in Salem, Indiana. He was happy with the life he was building, the life we was building with Thomas. He was comfortably housed, fed and he was safe. He knew his chances for success in life were improving. He had to admit he had come a long way from the day he was sitting on Sergeant Emerson's rough wagon seat. He had come a long way indeed!

Chapter 6

General McClellan was particularly fond of announcing, "All quiet along the Potomac." He felt it let the residents of the nation's capital sleep more easily. He believed it re-assured them. It was his way of saying, "Don't worry, the General has things under control." Thomas made good use of that quote in the fall of 1861.

"And why not?" Thomas thought. Both he and Jacob certainly shared that assessment. "And after all," he thought, "we know the state of things." And Thomas and Jacob did have a reasonably firm grasp on what was going on. Since their amazing visit to the War Department, they had continued to study the army and they were constantly impressed by what they saw. They were amazed by its growth. The now replaced General McDowell had taken 30,000 men to Bull Run a few short months ago. General McClellan's ranks had swelled to 150,000! And the mob that left D.C. for Manassas had been replaced by a professional army, the like of which the country, or maybe the world, had never seen.

General McClellan continued to train and inspect his army. No detail was too small boots, bridles, or belt buckles-the commanding general might stop and inspect anything. McClellan was demanding excellence.

One bright beautiful day, Thomas and Jacob joined their companions of the Second Rhode Island as the army prepared for a general inspection. It still amused Sergeant

Emerson that Thomas and Jacob were together. He rarely missed the chance to needle the two.

Thomas and Jacob watched as the sergeant prepared his men to pass muster. The soldiers jostled, laughed, complained, cursed and prepared to line up. "Got to polish up for the Big Bugs," one man called to Thomas. "Gonna see lots of chicken guts today!" added another. Sergeant Emerson called out, "Quit jawing; start toeing the line!"

As Thomas and Jacob moved out of the way, the men of the Second joined thousands and thousands of other Union soldiers. Line after line of the Army of the Potomac marched past their general. Thirty thousand civilians, including Thomas and Jacob, lined the road and cheered. Many of the soldiers sang as they marched.

What's that they're singing? asked Jacob

"Something called 'Marching Along', I believe." They listened as the men marched and sang:

"McClellan's our leader, he's gallant and strong,
For God and for country we are marching along."

Everyone agreed it was an impressive army indeed. McClellan had achieved a miracle. The capital was without doubt well protected. And things were quiet along the Potomac.

Thomas reported it all. He sent a steady stream of articles north to *The Constitutionalist*.

As summer gave way to fall, (it was fall only according to the calendar, Jacob contended, as he was still sweating in the Washington, D.C. heat) there was one War Department story that refused to go away. When Thomas first arrived in D.C., General Winfield Scott commanded of the army. He had been the commander for the last 20 years and was a well-respected man. He had served under every president from Jefferson to Lincoln. He had been serving his country since the War of 1812! One of his nicknames was the "Grand Old Man of the Army."

But he was also getting older and his health was suffering. He was after all, 74 years old. When the war first started, it was well known that he had actually asked one of his soldiers, a Colonel Robert E. Lee of Virginia, to take command of the Union forces. (Lee had declined and headed south.) So Thomas was not surprised when he began hearing rumors that Scott was going to retire. Thomas wrote the small story and sent it to New York.

But that was not the end of the story. Other rumblings began reaching Thomas' ears. He began hearing that the retirement was not one hundred percent voluntary. Voices whispered that some influential congressmen believed that Scott could no longer effectively lead, and they doubted his ability to end the rebellion. They wanted him out.

Thomas also learned that Scott had been asked to draw up a plan for winning the war and that that plan had not been well received by some. It was a long-term plan that called for capturing the Mississippi River and blockading the rebel states. There was no quick strike down to Richmond. It was going to be a long bloody war according to General Scott. This was certainly not the quick strike victory that many Northerners were clamoring for.

Then came the rumors that General McClellan himself was pushing Scott toward the door. Thomas instantly discarded this as empty gossip, but the rumors persisted. Thomas reluctantly concluded that he had to dig a bit into the story.

"Nonsense!" one War Department regular scoffed. "General McClellan has nothing but the highest respect for the Commanding General!" But other sources whispered a different story. It seemed that General Scott had initially welcomed the newcomer to the capital and that McClellan was respectful to his commander. But evidently, that relationship quickly soured, the voices told Thomas. Scott had come to believe that McClellan was arrogant, impudent, and disrespectful. Scott issued direct orders to McClellan, and those orders were ignored. In addition, he did not believe Mac had a plan for victory. He had become convinced Mac was moving much too slowly.

To top it off Scott heard that Mac was parading about town pronouncing Scott inept and outdated. Evidently Mac had changed his mind and now considered Scott an impediment. Insiders swore they had overheard Scott talk about charging Little Mac with insubordination.

Thomas was incredulous. He was stunned. "Jacob," he asked over lunch one day, "do you think that any of these stories hold the smallest crumb of truth? Or are they all the outright fabrications propagated by jealous men?"

Jacob pondered, chewing his mouthful of cheese and bread.

"Well, Sir," he finally said, "I've heard much the same. Many believe the only reason those orders weren't issued is that Scott feared it would hurt the army." Jacob reached for another piece of bread. "Or maybe it's because Little Mac has just gotten too powerful. Either way, I've heard about town that some serious bad blood has developed between the two."

The next evening Thomas joined some officers for dinner. He quickly put the matter directly to them. They just as quickly set about dissuading him. "Scott had already declared his intent to retire before Mac even got to the capital." one pointed out.

"And you know that Scott offered the command of the Union to Lee in April!" pushed another. "Little Mac didn't get here until after Bull Run!"

"Surely, Thomas," said yet a third, "you know that Scott suffers from rheumatism, among other things. Why the man is so overweight that he can no longer sit a horse. How could such a general conduct an inspection much less lead an army to victory?" he asked incredulously.

"But gentlemen," Thomas pressed "what about the clash between the two? What about the bad blood?"

"Much ado about nothing!" he was assured.

"Grossly exaggerated", responded another. "Thomas, you've been around army personnel long enough to know that some times words are spoken in the heat of the moment. Tempers momentarily flare and then settle down. Nothing serious to them, at all, I assure you."

Thomas had heard officers go at each other. He knew how quickly little things could blowup, only to be forgotten and forgiven minutes later. He was coming around to the opinion that there wasn't much of a story here. A bit of smoke perhaps, but no real fire. Thomas was mollified for the moment.

His next story reflected that thinking. It became Thomas' opinion that General Scott had served his country well, but it was time for a new leader. New blood was needed to defeat the Rebels.

Although it was currently quiet along the Potomac, the Rebels were still there. Right across the river, in fact. Rebels could be seen, setting up camps and aiming their cannon at the northern capital. True, they hadn't made a move, but "You don't plop cannons on hills unless you plan to use them!" Jacob liked to remind him. Thomas couldn't argue that fact.

One drizzly night in September, Thomas returned to the Dodge House to find Jacob buzzing with news.

"Did you hear about the New Jersey boys?"

"Uhm, no not really." He was sifting through his mail giving Jacob only part of his attention.

"Why, they lit out after the Rebels today!"

That news stopped Thomas in midstep. He had been out all day sniffing for stories and had not heard a single newsworthy thing. Now he comes home and Jacob has a scoop?

"Today? New Jersey boys? After the Rebels? What are you talking about, Jacob?"

Very full of himself and pleased that he had trumped Thomas, Jacob preened. He was in no big hurry now that he knew he had news that Thomas did not. "Well," he began in a slow drawl.

Thomas sharply struck his hand against the door frame.

"What do you know - exactly!! NOW! " he demanded, glaring at Jacob.

Jacob gave a little smile but started his tale.

"Truthfully, not all that much. I heard some New Jersey troops talking about a fracas...I think it was Munson's Hill, southwest of town. You know the hill with the Secesh flag flying? The hill you can see the Capitol dome from?"

Nodding quickly, Thomas said, "Yes, the one with the cannon."

"That's it. To hear these boys talk, some colonel ordered them out there to see how many Rebels were really there. Guess they found out! They got into a bit of a fracas. I know they took casualties."

Thomas had grabbed a notebook and was hurriedly scribbling. "How many casualties? New Jersey boys you say? Cannon fire?"

Jacob shook his head. "Now that's the surprising thing, to hear them tell it. They attacked, and were sharply met, but it was with rifle fire not cannon. No, Sir," he continued shaking his head. "Those cannons never let loose. They just sat on the hill, quiet and dark." Jacob laughed to himself. "Maybe those New Jersey boys skeedadled before the Rebs got a chance to load them cannons."

Thomas was ready to rush back out the door and dig for more information, but he realized it was too late, too dark, and he sadly realized he could file no story this evening.

The next day Thomas followed up Jacob's tale and got the full story. Evidently a New Jersey colonel had gotten tired of the Rebels sitting on Munson's Hill taking pot shots at, and hitting, his regiment. He decided to send a foray against the Confederates. "Let's give them a little lead and shake them off that hill," he said. Easier said than done. He quickly found out the Rebels were in strength on the hill, and that they were dug in. He also found out they were good marksmen. The New Jersey men took casualties, and the colonel pulled them back.

And, yes, Jacob had it right. The men had only experienced rifle fire. Those prominently placed cannons had remained strangely quiet.

After this brushup, however, quiet once again settled upon the Potomac. The Army of the Potomac went back to drilling; the Rebels went back to watching them.

Life continued on for Thomas and Jacob. Jacob was really impressing Thomas with his new-found learning. "Bright as a new penny", Thomas was fond of thinking. Of course he rarely shared his assessment with Jacob.

For his part Jacob found he enjoyed the chance to learn so many new things, both in his schooling and in his daily life around Washington. Of course, he never told Thomas that.

Jacob was becoming a regular sight and visitor among the men, around the camps, and around Washington.

Neither Thomas nor Jacob met Little Mac again although they would occasionally see him dashing about town. But they spent plenty of time at the War Department and made plenty of important contacts. The stories continued to flow. Thomas actually had money in his bank account, and Jacob had money in his pockets.

Then came October of 1861.

As the late summer days had passed, some members of Congress had become concerned that McClellan was using the army to drill but not to fight. When would that magnificent army find itself in battle? When would they march to Richmond? Did they plan to stay in Washington, D.C. all winter?

General McClellan responded by promising "I have no intention of putting the army into winter quarters. I mean the campaign will be short, sharp, and decisive." He would wave his hand toward Virginia and promise "We will soon be on those people," but he did not move. His words said one thing; his actions another.

McClellan complained about the "interference in his plans" from people who "were far less knowledgable" but the pressure continued. Pressure was placed on President Lincoln, who in turn, passed the urgency on to his general.

McClellan may not have wanted to make a move, but he was smart enough to realize that some kind of move was necessary. He felt the president's hand in the middle of his back. So to relieve that pressure, in late October, he decided to make a move. He sent for General Stone.

He directed Stone to "go evaluate the enemy's strength." Specifically he ordered Stone to Leesburg, Virginia to investigate the condition and status of Confederate Colonel Nathan Evan's troops. He was to "possibly draw them out, to determine their intentions." Orders in hand, General Stone left for Leesburg.

General Stone and his men made the 40-some mile trip upriver. Once there he sent men to reconnoiter the situation. Sadly an inexperienced captain was sent out to explore. The captain excitedly reported that he had found an undefended Rebel camp ripe for the picking. Sadly for the Army of the Potomac, the Captain was wrong. He had not found an undefended camp. He had found a camp of boys from Mississippi, soldiers who were dug in and ready for a fight. His information led Union troops to disaster. The Rebels drove the unprepared, outnumbered Yankees back across the Potomac. By the end of the engagement, the Yankees had suffered almost a thousand casualties.

By chance, Thomas was at the War Department that October day. Afternoon poker games at the War Department had become an item. They were thoroughly illegal of course, but when the cat is away…Thomas sat with five officers that afternoon, sharing his money with them. Suddenly the telegraphs sprang to life, and began chattering away. Poker was forgotten as the officers rushed to their posts. Telegram after telegram arrived. The men in the War Department began to get information about General Stone's expedition to Leesburg.

Depression filled the room. The men did not understand what was going on or why the Union was losing. Stunned men milled about trying to understand the situation.

Thomas saw the situation as an opportunity. Grabbing one card playing acquaintance he begged, "Let me have the jist of those messages. Just the broad outline. No classified details. Just let me get the news of this action to the people." Without a word the shocked captain handed Thomas some of the telegraphs. Basically they told Thomas:

11:00am - General Stone's troops had engaged the enemy.

1:00pm -The fighting was intense.

2:00pm - The Union was being thrown back.

4:00pm casualties high. Defeat looks certain.

Thomas ran through the telegrams reading as fast as he was able. Then he grabbed pen and paper and sat at a small round table in the corner of the room. His pen scratched noisily as he composed his story. He was deep in thought when suddenly that pen was wrenched from his hand. Stunned, Thomas looked up to see that one of his poker-playing companions was holding his dripping pen.

"Look here, Thomas, you can write your article, but I need to make sure you understand General McClellan has nothing to do with this tragedy. You must make it clear that he had nothing to do with ordering any kind of attack!" The man's hands shook as he spoke. A small shower of ink drops stained Thomas' work.

Thomas looked at the man in surprise. "What on earth do you mean? The general is not leading this fight? Why not?"

"Lord no, Thomas. He's right here in D.C. He sent General Stone to reconnoiter, not to attack entrenched Rebel troops. There was never meant to be an attack. I mean, man, think of it. These prove it!" He said, pointing at the telegraphs. "Hundreds dead, wounded or captured! This is a disaster! This is what happens when you let inexperienced officers fight with untrained men! Disaster!" he repeated in anguish.

Thomas nodded quickly gently taking the pen back. He assured the agitated captain that his report would be very fair to General McClellan. No blame would come to the General from Thomas' article. He returned to his work.

Thomas hated that he was sharing the news of a Union loss, but he was elated that he was sharing the news. This was big news and it appeared that he was the only reporter who had it. There was not another newsman in sight. Thomas was about to scoop every single other paper in the country! This news had to get out and fast.

Thomas also hated to admit it, but he felt that he needed this article. His last few stories had been fine, but they were hitting the same notes - all ready, but all quiet. Now he could send in real news; now he could report action. The pen continued its scratching across the paper.

Not less than fifteen minutes later, Thomas had the first report of the Battle of Leesburg heading to the *Constitutionalist*.

Thomas rushed back to the Dodge House and excitedly shared the news with Jacob. "This should land us above the fold!" he exclaimed. "This should earn some inches!"

"Congratulations, Sir! Outstanding work! Well done!" Jacob gushed. He paused for a few seconds and then asked "Now what's for dinner?"

What neither of them knew at that minute was that while Thomas had his scoop, he also had made his second serious journalistic mistake.

Chapter 7

The sun rose the next day ushering in a beautiful fall day. As he prepared for breakfast, Thomas was basking in his success. His story had been accepted by his editor. He had received that confirmation via wire last night. Copies of the New York *Constitutionalist* would be on the streets that afternoon, and Thomas had no doubt his article would be front and center. After all, this was big news, big news, and best of all, he had an exclusive. The *Constitutionalist* would lead the way! All because of him. "Yes," Thomas mused, "life is good."

Or at least it was until Jacob returned with their breakfast and a newspaper. "You know who Edward Baker is?" Jacob asked, almost before he closed the door.

"Uhmm, yes a congressman I believe." Thomas thought a minute more. "A senator I believe from…the uhmm, somewhere out west?"

Jacob pulled a folded newspaper from his jacket pocket. "According to this morning's *Washington National Republican*," he said, "he's a senator who *was* also a colonel in the army. According to them, he *was* a personal friend of the president. Also according to them, he was also killed yesterday afternoon in the battle at Leesburg."

Thomas stopped cold. No one had mentioned a colonel's death yesterday! Certainly no one had mentioned a senator's death! And this senator was a personal friend of the president? Suddenly, Thomas' day didn't seem quite so bright. Suddenly his scoop didn't look so wonderful.

How could this be? How could he have missed such an important fact? Was Jacob's information true? He wracked his memory, trying to remember every detail of the telegrams. Had he been so hasty he had missed this crucial fact? Had this even been reported? How had he missed this? A black mood began drizzling rain on his beautiful day.

His stomach roiled as he tried to think. For a minute or so he actually thought he was going to be sick right in the middle of the room. He grabbed the back of a chair steeling himself not to vomit.

He soon realized, however, what was done, was done. There was nothing he could do about yesterday's story now. In minutes it would be on the streets of New York.

The only thing to do now was write a second story, a new story, adding this new information.

After a few more minutes hands pressed against his eyes, Thomas spoke, "Well, no choice but to try and clean this mess up."

"Yes, Sir", Jacob replied. "What do we do?"

"I have to get another story on the wire, a second story, a part two. We've got to have more information." Visions of losing his job swirled. The vomit rose in his throat again. Thomas closed his eyes, willing it away.

"Fine, Sir. How do we set about getting that new story?"

Thomas opened his eyes and began creating a plan.

As had become their practice, the two agreed to separate. Thomas would make a more formal, frontal assault on the War Department. Jacob would take a more circular approach, soaking up information and details where he could.

Jacob grabbed his hat and made his way out. Thomas made his return to the War Department.

There, the change was immediately apparent. Yesterday he had merely nodded to the sentries and wandered in. Today his way was barred. The sentries quickly stopped him loudly pronouncing, "Authorized personnel on official business-only!" Thomas almost tossed a cutting response at the two men, but their look caused him to swallow his smart comment. The men were serious but they appeared to be scared. Equally importantly, their rifles now had bright shiny new bayonets attached. Thomas was sure those blades had not been there yesterday!

"Clearly the world had changed in the last 24 hours." Thomas muttered to no one. "Apparently no afternoon poker games are going to be held this day."

Thomas turned, took a few steps down and to the side. He stood there, considering his situation. As he did so, a flow of men pushed in and out the door. They passed him without so much as a glance. "Oh what a difference a day makes." he sighed to himself. Even when he recognized one or two past sources, they hurried past without a word. One man silently shook his head at Thomas. Evidently no one wanted to be seen talking to a newspaper reporter today.

Thomas decided to try and find someone who would vouch for him. Finally a major Thomas knew walked up. Thomas literally grabbed the man's arm as he walked by. "Don't know what help I can be," the major said with a tone of regret. "This place is a madhouse. Everyone is making sure there is no way they get blamed for this disaster. Couldn't possibly walk you in today!"

The major's assessment was spot on. No one had time to talk with Thomas. Most folks weren't rude, but they weren't welcoming either. Past history didn't seem to matter today.

Over the next hour Thomas continued to try to gain access to information. A couple of acquaintances made cryptic comments, but that was about all. Finally, one lieutenant colonel who had enjoyed more than a few of the drinks Thomas had purchased handed him a folded piece of paper. "6:00 - Raleigh's Tavern" it read. Ruefully Thomas thought to himself, "Maybe I'll get more information there. Or maybe I'll just have a lighter purse when we're finished." Either way he decided, he had little choice. He wasn't getting any more information at the War Department this day, that much was clear.

Luckily Jacob was having more success. Jacob first headed for his old stomping grounds, the Second Ohio. He wandered the camp hoping to find men talking about yesterday. He heard earfuls. The first thing he learned was that evidently the battle had a new name - Ball's Bluff.

"Disaster," grumbled one man as he loaded a wagon.

"How did they think they would get across that damn river without enough boats, anyway?" asked a second.

"And how did they think they would get back?" replied his friend.

"A useless slaughter!" barked another. "Bodies still floating downriver, right over yonder!" he exclaimed, thrusting an arm out toward the Potomac, "Right now, right as we speak!" Jacob decided to take the man at his word and not venture to the river. He did not need to see floating bodies. Instead he left the Ohio boys and headed over to the Second Rhode Island. He was hoping to come across Sergeant Emerson. After a short search through his old camp, he found the man, busily cleaning his musket. The Sergeant was in a bad mood, "Bad business, Jacob. Bad business."

"But what happened Sergeant? What's the rub?"

Sergeant Emerson put aside his musket. He looked around before answering the boy. "Way I hear it, it was Baker's inexperience that got him killed."

"Senator Baker? What do you mean?"

"From what I hear, Baker pushed across the river without doing any recon. He didn't know what he was getting into; didn't know how he might get out." Emerson sadly shook his head, "Poor soldiering."

Jacob looked shocked at the statement,

"Well, now hold on!" Emerson said, reacting to Jacob's look. "I'm sorry he's dead. I'm sorry anyone's dead. He may have been a fine senator and a good friend to the president! I hear the president even named a son after him. But the man had no experience as a soldier. He got himself in a bad place and he paid the price. And that's the God's truth, sorry to say." He spat on the ground. "Poor soldiering!" he repeated.

"But why didn't we hear about the senator's death yesterday during the battle?" pressed Jacob.

"He wasn't killed until almost sunset, way I hear it. It was deep dark by the time we heard about it last night."

That made sense to Jacob. "So what's next?" he asked Emerson. "Figure everyone's moving toward Leesburg; starting the action up in a big way?"

The sergeant gave him a sour look. "No, I reckon we all get back to drillinn' and try to forget this even happened." This surprised Jacob a bit, but he had been around the sergeant too long not to take him at his word.

Thomas was equally surprised by the news he received at his 6:00 meeting.

"Thomas!" the lieutenant colonel cried, jerking his thumb in the general direction of the War Department. "What a madhouse, glad to escape the place!" He reached for the drink that sat waiting on the table. "Thanks for the drink. Exactly what is needed on this day!" He took a long swallow.

Wiping his mustache with the back of his hand, he continued. "No one wants responsibility for this fiasco! Everyone is running away as fast and hard as they can!" He took another swallow.

"But what happened," Thomas asked, "What happened to the army and what happened to Baker?"

"What happened to both is that inexperienced people, ill equipped to do a job, suddenly found themselves in deep water, water way over their heads. Thomas, none of this was supposed to happen! The army isn't ready! The men aren't ready, the nation isn't ready! I mean look at them, man. The proof's in the pudding! Look what happened once they were let out on their own. They were never supposed to fight. Little Mac sent them to get information, not to get people killed! If there was to be a real battle, don't you think the commanding general himself would have been there?"

"Compelling points", Thomas admitted. "But then," he said pointing his beer glass at the man, "when will we be ready? I mean, haven't we been drilling and reviewing and parading for months? Didn't Mac basically say Beauregard was finished winning battles?"

Thomas knew he had the man there. McClellan had said it, and Thomas had quoted him. The General had said, "I flatter myself that Beauregard has gained his last victory. The people call upon me to save the country. I must save it and I cannot respect anything that is in the way. I was called to it, my previous life seems to have been unwittingly directed to this great end." Word for word it had appeared in The *Constitutionalist*.

"Yes, of course he said it! And of course you know it, Thomas, since you reported it!" He paused to take another long pull at his beer.

"Yes, we've drilled. But taking a green mob and making them into an effective army is almost a magical trick! Look, we've got a green army that is outnumbered maybe 2 to 1, maybe 3 or 4 to 1. And while we're green men, we're outnumbered by experienced fighters. Those people have been training for his fight for years! We're trying to build an army from the ground up.

And besides, winter is moving in. Have you seen this weather?" he gestured outside at the cold rain that was falling. "Turning all roads to mud and then to ice. No, Thomas, no one can fight in winter."

"Napoleon did," Thomas blurted, almost before he could stop himself.

"Ah, yes, Napoleon, thank you for making my case for me. Indeed Napoleon did indeed try to ignore the weather and fight a winter campaign." The man shook his finger in Thomas' face. "And look what happened to him! Destroyed! Destroyed by the Russian Winter, the Russian Army and that General Winter! Is that what you want? Do you truly want another disaster like this one or the disaster that was Bull Run? No, no Thomas my boy," he leaned over to pat Thomas on the arm, "we'll move when we are ready to end this rebellion in one decisive, massive victory." He leaned back and smiled at Thomas. "That'll give you something to write about, heh?"

And as it turned out, both Jacob's and Thomas' sources were right. As Sergeant Emerson predicted, the Army of the Potomac ignored Lewisburg and went right back to training. And Thomas' companion was right that winter quarters were about to be set up. Thomas reported both facts. Things had indeed returned to quiet all along the Potomac.

There was a minor flurry of attention when General Scott's retirement day came around. This was the day General George B. McClellan was being given command of all the Union Armies. This gave Thomas a small jolt, reminding him of the rumors he had heard about Mac pushing Scott out of office. He felt a second jolt when he heard what President Lincoln had told the new leader of the Union forces. Rumor had it the president had warned the new commanding general, "the supreme command of the army will entail a vast labor upon you." McClellan reportedly smiled and responded, "I can do it all."

But Thomas' qualms were somewhat satisfied when he learned that General McClellan, his staff and a squad of cavalry rose at 4:00 am to pay their respects to General Scott. They accompanied the retiring general through the darkness and rain to the train station. Evidently there, the two men exchanged their respects. That gesture made Thomas more sure that General McClellan was blameless.

The general did not seem blameless a few days later, though. One day, the Union troops around Munson's Hill, site of the New Jersey's boys engagement, woke up to a strange sight. They could see rebel cannon on the hill quite clearly, but they could not see any rebels. None. This made no sense. Cannon without cannoneers? Why on earth would rebels suddenly go into hiding?

The Union men cautiously made their way up the hill to find out. They had made this trip once before and remembered it well, but this time was different. They did not indeed find the first rebel. They were gone. The northern men were stunned and confused.

They could not figure out why the rebels would leave and they were even more puzzled that apparently, they had left their cannon behind.

Then the truth became clear. The New Jersey boys were not staring at cannon, as they had believed, they were staring at logs, logs painted pitch black. Wagon wheels were nailed to the logs to complete the image. "Well, Damn me boys," cried an astonished Union private, "It's a Quaker gun!" Clearly no Union soldier had been in danger of taking fire from this.

Publicly, the War Department shrugged the incident off as "one of those things." not everyone was buying that story however and some congressmen, already displeased with Mac's pace began to seriously grumble. What was he doing with this new Army of the Potomac? What was his plan?

Thomas was very upset by the discovery, but his unhappiness was not with Little Mac. His lay in another direction. He was upset because another New York reporter placed the story first. Thomas was clearly in second place in this race. And second place, Thomas knew, was not a place his publisher enjoyed. He certainly would not be paying Thomas for any second place finishes.

Thomas was upset again a few night's later. He was enjoying a late dinner with a few army acquaintances. Toward the end of the rather lengthy meal, one man leaned over and in a low, confidential voice said, "I don't know if

I should be telling you this, but I feel I need to. You might want to take a little more care with your stories."

Thomas gave the man a very surprised look. "Care? Whatever do you mean?"

"You may want to be careful." he warned. "In some corners, your articles have become seen as being very pro-McClellan."

"They aren't!" Thomas sternly snapped. "My articles are pro-Army of the Potomac!"

The officer pushed back. "And to whom do you give the credit?"

"Hmmmm," Thomas admitted. "I do suppose that I give Mac most of the credit for that! Remember, I was with the army that fought at Bull Run! We are nothing like that now! We have a trained professional army and Mac has done most of the work . Doesn't he deserve the credit? What's wrong with giving credit where credit is due? Besides who would be unhappy with me being pro McClellan or pro Union Army? Outside of the rebels I mean!" He gave the officer a bit of a mean look. "Or do we care what they think these days?"

The man looked around as if he were afraid of being overheard. He shook his head. "You don't understand. You don't want the committee's attention and I'm afraid you are close to drawing it."

Now Thomas was both puzzled and irked. "What committee? Why would I care how people interpret my articles?"

"Not people." the man quickly rejoined. "The Joint Committee on the Conduct of the War. Haven't you heard of it?"

"Well…"Thomas hedged. Truth be told he had heard of it, but he hadn't paid it much thought. There were so many congressional committees. They seemed to all demand attention. Thomas had come to ignore them.

Sensing his attitude, his dinner companion pushed, "You'd better not ignore this one, I can tell you. They are serious, Thomas and they have some serious power. They are unhappy with the state of the war, unhappy with our losses and I think they are looking for someone to blame. Personally, I want nothing to do with them and I hope to high heaven they never hear my name!"

Thomas had no response to that. But it did give him a strange chill to think about being under the gaze of a hostile congressional committee.

Chapter 8

The Constitution declares the president to be commander in chief of the armed forces. It gives Congress the power to declare war. And perhaps even more importantly, it gives Congress, specifically the House of Representatives, the power of the purse. The president may direct the war, but the Congress pays for it.

This bit of political science came into focus sharply in the late fall of 1861. For the first few months of the war, during a special summer session, the Congress basically provided Mr. Lincoln with all that he requested. But as summer gave way to fall, that was beginning to change. Some members began questioning the war effort and war results. Some members of Congress did not share the soldiers' high regard for General McClellan. Some members worried that he was slow to act. When President Lincoln promoted McClellan, appointing him chief of all forces, these congressmen became very worried. Feeling it was their duty, they shared those worries with the president.

Mr. Lincoln listened politely, but he assured the concerned congressmen that General McClellan was the best choice for the job. Some men walked away unconvinced. Some began to worry about Mr. Lincoln's prowess and his ability to conduct the war.

A few congressmen met unofficially to discuss the situation. They began to ask if their summer decisions had been prudent. They began asking pointed questions. A few congressmen came to the conclusion that they had been remiss in their duties. They decided they had left too much to the president. They decided it was time to change that. It was time they helped shape the war effort. "One million dollars a day is being spent on this war," thundered one, "that ought to entitle us to some answers!"

What finally pushed them into real action? It was probably a combination of factors. Weeks of McClellan pronouncements promising action, followed by weeks of nothing more than drills and inspections. Quaker guns were found to be paralyzing Union troops. The disaster at Ball's Bluff. All these helped the congressional demand for action slowly gain momentum.

First, Congressman Roscoe Conkling, a Republican from New York, asked for a congressional inquiry into the Ball's Bluff disaster. Then Michigan Republican Zachariah Chandler asked the Congress to investigate both Ball's Bluff and Bull Run. Why did the Union lose these battles, the congressman wanted to know? Why was the Union losing the war? Congress wanted answers.

Accordingly, in early December, the congress voted to create a joint committee on the conduct of the war. The committee would consist of three senators and four representatives. The committee was granted the power to "inquire into the conduct of the present war and to send for persons and papers." The committee announced its intentions to get answers to the question, "Why was the rebellion not ended?"

One of their first acts, was to formally return to the office of the President. Lincoln had heard from some of them before. Now he would hear from then again - formally.

The president understood the system. He understood that Congress provided political support. He also firmly understood that the Congress provided the money he so desperately needed to put down the rebellion. Accordingly, when they called again, Mr. Lincoln listened closely. The president's aide took copious notes.

Again, many of the congressional questions centered on General George McClellan.

"General McClellan says he can do it all? I haven't seen him do anything! When is he going to act?"

"All quiet? All quiet? Why is it so dad-gummed quiet? With eleven states in rebellion, he expects us to be pleased he is doing nothing?"

"Why have we lost all the battles we have fought? Why is the South winning?"

"Richmond is a mere 90 miles south of here! 90 short miles! Why don't we hear troops marching south instead of tromping all around Washington undergoing inspections?"

"Why has General McClellan not moved the army against the rebellious southern states?"

"How long does he plan to wait before taking action against the Confederacy?"

"Is the general competent?"

"Is the general lucid?"

"Should the general be replaced?"

Mr. Lincoln listened to it all. He promised to look into each question and get back to the committee. As they prepared to walk out of the room, Mr. Lincoln issued one last thought. He cautioned them that he was sure General McClellan was still, at least for this minute, the best man for the job. Nonetheless, he promised to again talk with the general and get back to them.

True to his word, President Lincoln scheduled a meeting with General McClellan. Neither man wanted the meeting. The atmosphere was tense.

First of all, the president assured the general, he had no greater supporter than Mr. Lincoln. However, others need some reassuring. General McClellan was unimpressed. "The buzzing of busybodies and gadflies!" he exclaimed. Later that evening when he took pen to paper to write his wife about the meeting, he shared with her how unhappy he was with the interference. "I can't tell you how disgusted I am become with these wretched politicians."

That afternoon with the president, however, he was more diplomatic. His words were softer, but he made it

clear that he considered Congress to be interring with his
army.

"That may be," the president acknowledged, "but
those men need some answers. They are not going away.
They must be told something. Remember, General, they do
control the purse!"

McClellan answered, "I intend to be careful and do
as well as possible. Please tell them that." He continued
telling the president that he was in the midst of creating a
successful plan that would end the rebellion.

It was true that McClellan had a plan in mind. He
called it the Urbana Plan. It was true that McClellan
actually intended to move, but it was also true that he
would move when all was ready and not a minute before.
And he certainly was not going to move on the word of
politicians-not the word of Congress, the committee, the
cabinet, not on the word of the president himself!

McClellan left the meeting secure that he had said
all he needed to say. He was sure the matter was ended.
He was wrong. It was not.

The president was also sure-he was sure the
committee would not be satisfied with McClellan's
response. True to his word, he shared the bulk of
McClellan's message with the committee. He was astute
enough not to share the general's exact language nor his
sentiments about the congressmen.

And as Lincoln predicted, the committee members
were not mollified, not by a long shot. "Fine", they seemed
to say. "We tried it your way. We'll now go a different
way." They promptly announced that they would call

General McClellan himself in front of the committee. They would put their questions directly to the commander himself. They would be provided with answers.

Before the committee summoned McClellan however, he took the opportunity to meet again with the President. On December 10, 1861, McClellan met with Lincoln to explain his Urbana Plan. He laid out the major components for the president.

"As you know, Mr. President, since the disaster at Bull Run, we have been drilling, training, expanding our army. It is now improved. We are now ready to move."

"As you also know, since that disastrous battle, the rebels under General Johnson have been occupying Northern Virginia. They have planted themselves firmly between my army and Richmond."

"As I've also shared with you, the rebels greatly outnumber my forces. Some experts feel we are outnumbered three to one! If we were to launch a frontal assault against a larger, entrenched army, we would surely lose. Nay, we would be destroyed!" he said vehemently. He stared hard at Lincoln as if daring the president to contradict his facts. "It is a certainty of war, Sir!"

Lincoln listened without comment.

"However, Sir," McClellan continued, "there is another way." McClellan moved to a nearby table and unrolled a large detailed map. "Let me show you, Sir." He placed a forefinger on the map. "Here is the current position of the rebels." He drew a semi-circle on the map, indicating the rebel's position. "Instead of plunging heedlessly against entrenched forces with great loss of life,

I have created a plan with a far higher degree of success and a plan that guarantees far fewer casualties."

McClellan continued. He planned on enlisting the navy to help him float his army down the Potomac and into the Chesapeake Bay. At the mouth of the Rappahannock River, he would swing westward heading up the Rappahannock River. McClellan's finger drew the route as he talked. "This will allow us to get behind the rebel forces, avoiding a head on attack completely. We'll land here," he said tapping a spot on the river "and that will place us between the rebels and Richmond. They will be cut off!

The general's voice rose a notch as he continued. "We will find the high ground. They will be forced to attack us, on ground of our choosing. They will be the ones attacking an entrenched army!" McClellan took a deep breath and plunged on. "We will win the battle and win the war. The rebels will be defeated!"

The president had listened to every word but it was clear he did not share his general's fervor for the plan. "How would the Army of the Potomac receive supplies? How long would this take? And most importantly, would not this plan leave the capital open to rebel attack? While you float down the river away from the capital, what will stop the rebels from pushing right in?"

McClellan had answers, lots of them. But those answers did not convince the president. Eventually, however, Lincoln agreed that there was, at least, a plan to discuss. And most importantly, the president could tell the committee McClellan was planning on moving. It was more than he had had before.

The general may have really hoped to move quickly and decisively. However as December days passed, McClellan realized he would be doing neither. He was not going to be able to move his forces during 1861. He wrote his wife, "I am doing all I can to get the campaign moved before winter sets in, but it now begins to seem as if we were condemned to a winter of inactivity. If it is so, the fault will not be mine: there will be consultation for my conscience, even if the world at large never knows it." Strangely, while he shared this assessment with his wife, he did not share it with the president. As far as the president knew, Little Napoleon still planned on moving soon.

McClellan did not move. His assessment was correct. The rains came, the roads turned into mud. The army could not march or float to fight the rebels in such weather. The Army of the Potomac would not fight in 1861. This information, when finally delivered to the White House, deeply frustrated President Lincoln.

The information infuriated some committee members. Evidently, McClellan's inaction proved to be the last straw. On December 22, the Committee announced it would begin an interrogation of General McClellan. He would be forced to appear. He would be forced to explain and defend his so-called efforts to win the war.

That news set Washington buzzing, Thomas and Jacob included. They sat in their new rooms at the Dodge House sharing dinner.

"Interrogate General McClellan?" Thomas huffed. "How dare they? They sit in their grand offices, stroll their grand halls and do nothing. Little Mac, designed, built and trained this army!"

"Hmmm," Jacob responded, chewing on a very large bite.

"And what do they hope to accomplish?" Thomas steamed on. "They are keeping the general from his duties! His duty to defeat the rebels! What are those wooly headed Congressmen thinking?" He stabbed at his plate, righteous with indignation.

"Hmmmmmm," Jacob said around an even larger bite of food.

Thomas jerked up and looked at his companion. "You're defending the congress?"

"Hmmmmmmmm."

Thomas put down his fork and stared at his companion. "You are not making yourself clear, Jacob! Or is that your intent? Are you being troublesome on purpose? Obtuse?"

Obtuse? Jacob shook his head at that word. Then he said, "Well, I guess it's true that he did create the army…"

"There!" Thomas quickly jumped in. "Thank you! That's exactly why this is such a load of cow manure…"

Jacob interrupted right back, continuing his thought, "but I guess I hear a lot of people comment on the fact that Bull Run was six months ago." He gave Thomas a steady look.

"Six months? Six months?" Thomas paused, obviously confused by this train of thought. "Well, what of it? So what?"

"Well, yes, six months." Jacob said. "Six months. Some folk say that much inaction might give the rebels the idea we have no interest in reuniting the country."

"Now that's preposterous!" Thomas thundered, "First of all, we have not been inactive…" but then Jacob's words sunk in. Six months? Had it really been six months? Thomas did the math in his head. He realized Jacob was absolutely correct, June to December. Thomas had not really realized there had been that much of a delay. He stuttered, "…not inaction. After all," he said, regaining his composure a bit, "it takes time to build an army. I'm sure every day of those six months was badly needed. Remember," he said shaking a finger for emphasis, "we started with an untrained mob. That army needed to be trained. The general could not have moved an untrained mob of men against an organized opponent, an opponent I remind you that outnumbers our forces, probably as much as three to one!" Thomas leaned back, sure he was back on solid ground. "That ought to settle his hash!" he thought.

Instead of appearing subdued, Jacob leaned over, moved the food on his plate and forked another large bite. "Hmmmm." as he said as he chewed. Finally he finished the bite and pointed the empty fork at Thomas. "Let me ask you something about that-a couple of things actually." Now he raised a single finger in the air, tilting it at Thomas. "First of all, before you go off half cocked, this comes from the schooling you're insisting I receive!"

Thomas scowled at him but said nothing.

Jacob continued, "One day we were doing sums and studying problems when the teacher gave us this one." Assuming the role of teacher, he pointed at Thomas. "How many states remain in the Union today?"

"Twenty two." Thomas answered in bit of a snotty tone.

"Correct. And how many states went south?"

"Eleven and before you ask another obvious question, there are three border states, everyone knows this."

"Oh they do, do they? Fine, then answer me this Mr. Everybody knows this! Why if we have twice as many states as the Rebs, are we so all fired ready to believe that they have twice as many men as we do?"

That question literally pushed Thomas back into his chair. He had never heard the question presented that way and it stunned him.

Seeing his reaction, Jacob pushed on. "Let me give you some more to chew on." The fork came stabbing back in Thomas' direction. "Now the folks you sent me to to get educated, those fine folks, they figure there are about 22 million people in the northern states. The teacher, he also figures the south has no more than 10 million people, maybe less. Maybe even only 9 million. And he also figures thousands, maybe hundred of thousands, heck maybe even a million of those people are slaves. I don't know, I've never counted. But I do figure those slaves surely won't be found in the rebel army in any great number. By my figuring if we take the slaves out of the equation, and let's say there are a million of them, that leaves the south with 8-9 million people. We've got 22 million in the north with no slaves. So I ask you again, where do these great rebel numbers come from?"

Pouncing further, Jacob asked, "Did they start with some secret army I didn't know about? I mean didn't this war start at the same time for both sides? How come they end up with an organized army when we got a mob of untrained boys, to use some people's quote?" He tossed Thomas' words right back at him. He accompanied them with a very satisfied smile.

Thomas sat silently. He had never stopped to put that information together. As he listened it hit him that Jacob was basically right. He was embarrassed that he had never come to such an obvious conclusion himself. He had no ready answer to Jacob's points.

He cleared his throat. "I guess it could seem that way…" he began. But then he stopped. Jacobs points were still ratcheting around his brain. Could the boy be right? It was indeed six months. The north did indeed have a larger population. Had he been missing something so obvious all this time? Thomas suddenly developed a very queasy feeling in his stomach. Had he been misreading everything? What else was he wrong about? With a sinking feeling of neglect, he realized he needed to do a much more thorough job of researching and especially, a more thorough job of thinking. He needed better information and he needed to analyze it much more closely.

Meanwhile, a few blocks away on Capitol Hill, members of the committee were also giving matters a hard second thought. They had listened to the answers President Lincoln provided. They decided they found them wanting. Accordingly, they decided to order General McClellan to appear before the committee forthwith.

The general did not appear. Instead he sent word. The general, it was announced had taken to his sick bed. At first, it was reported that he had a bad cold. Then his doctor announced that the general was suffering from typhoid.

"Typhoid, hey?" scoffed one committee member. "I was told he had a cold. The doctors can't tell the difference between the two?"

"You don't believe the doctor?" another queried.

"Who is paying the doctor?" he responded.

"Or" a third man chimed in, "a better question might be, who commands the doctor? With a cold, we could command the general's presence. With typhoid, his appearance must be postponed." He looked hard at the two men and pointedly asked, "Now what do you believe is really going on here?"

Up Pennsylvania Avenue, at 1600, Mr. Lincoln had finished with his serious thinking. He had come to a conclusion. "The bottom is out of the tub!" he announced as he walked into the room.

"I beg your pardon, Sir?" a very startled Quartermaster General M.C. Meigs asked.

Mister Lincoln had walked into the quartermaster's office unannounced. Now he plopped down on the divan across from Meig's desk. "General, what shall we do? The people are impatient: Chase has no money and he tells me he can raise no more: the General of the Army has typhoid fever. The bottom is out of the tub. What shall I do?"

Meigs sat silently, staring back at the president. He made no reply. He had no answers for his president.

And 1861 slide into 1862.

Chapter 9

Christmas had been enjoyed, New Year celebrated, and 1862 was underway. Thomas was sure that the new year would be a much different year and he told Jacob as much. "Things may have been all quiet along the Potomac in 1861," he said "but I am sure events will be getting underway in 1862!" He didn't say it but it was understood that Thomas was determined to cover each and every one of those events for the *Constitutionalist*.

His first story broke a mere ten days into the year. President Lincoln was taking action!

Quartermaster Meigs had come to the president. "Sir, if General McClellan truly does have typhoid, he will be recovering for at least six weeks."

The president looked at his quartermaster. "Meigs, you're right. And we can't afford to wait that long!" Mr. Lincoln paused and then said, almost to himself, "No Sir! This year we are going to have action!"

Lincoln leaned his long frame back, chair creaking and crossed his fingers across his chest. " You know, General, last week I met with General McClellan and though he was sick, he would not put someone else in even temporary command."

"If I may Mr. President. Why not call on General McClellan's top commanders and ask them to present a plan for action? If he is truly to be out six weeks, most probably one of them is going to have to take over."

The President's face lit up. He clearly liked Meigs' idea. Within minutes he had summoned the officers to the meeting. When they arrived, the president got straight to the point. "Gentlemen, we need to pursue the war. If General McClellan is not going to use the army, I would like to borrow it." Stunned by the comment, the generals made no reply.

That last comment was made in a private meeting at the White House, yet the quote soon swept around Washington, D.C. like a hurricane! The generals may not have responded to it, but others did. Thomas certainly made good use of it in his article. He reported that Lincoln had asked the generals to come up with a plan to take the Army of the Potomac into the field. He had given them 48 hours and the following meeting was already scheduled. It seemed that the president was intent on using the army, with or without its commanding general.

McClellan's two top commanders, General McDowell of Bull Run fame and General Franklin had differing ideas. General McDowell favored a land march toward Manassas; General Franklin supported General McClellan's Urbana Plan.

Lincoln listened carefully to both men, then ordered them to continue their thoughts and be ready to present their ideas at the next meeting. Over the next two days the men met, trying to form a plan for action. Finally, they came to a consensus. The overland route would be easier to put into action. They agreed it was the plan they would pursue.

What happened next remained something of a Washington, D.C. mystery. Thomas never exactly found out who, though he had his theories, but someone visited General McClellan's sick bed. With some well-placed comments, they planted a seed. "They're plotting to take your army away! They want you dead!" McClellan came to the conclusion that if he wanted to keep the Army of the Potomac, he needed to take action.

Stunning Lincoln, his generals, and the entire capital, McClellan left his sick bed and appeared at the next day's meeting. He was sickly, pale and obviously in some distress. But he was there determined to keep his army. With some obvious disdain for his officers, he convinced Lincoln there was no more need of a meeting. McClellan had a plan, and he was happy to share it with the president.

Sadly, once McClellan started talking, Lincoln realized it was once again the Urbana plan. The President still did not like the plan. He hadn't liked it the first time it was presented. But this time, he was ready. He gave McClellan a list of of specific questions. "If you give me satisfactory answers...I shall gladly yield my plan to yours."

McClellan jumped at the chance. "You shall have your answers, Sir," and with that the meeting ended. McClellan was back in charge.

McClellan was a gifted organizer and planner. He was a student of war. So it was not a suprise that when he returned to President Lincoln he had a complete list of answers. He had done his homework. He emerged from the meeting victorious. The president had to agree that McClellan had superior military knowledge. It appeared McClellan had an answer for each one of Lincoln's concerns. As the meeting adjourned, the president had not approved McClellan's plan, but neither had he ordered it abandoned. McClellan left thinking he had avoided a major disaster. His plan would go forward.

General McClellan may have had a plan, but President Lincoln was not finished prodding the Army of the Potomac into action. On January 11th, Lincoln took another giant step. He reassigned his first Secretary of War, Simon Cameron to an ambassadorship in Russia. Then he asked Democrat Edwin Stanton to become the next Secretary of War. That news shocked Washington.

"McClellan will love that!" Thomas chortled to Jacob as they discussed the bombshell. "What an odd choice! I wonder if Lincoln knows what we know?"

"And what exactly do we know?" Jacob asked.

"We know that McClellan and Stanton are friends. When McClellan was looking for a place to hide from President Lincoln he went to Stanton's house. I also have a sneaking suspicion that Stanton visited McClellan at his sick bed!"

"It's also rumored that Stanton has said some very disparaging things about the President. Yeeesss, I think this will be a favorable turn of events for the General."

"Tomorrow, Jacob, we are off to Capital Hill. Time to find out what our duly elected representatives think about this situation." The Senate did, after all, have to confirm the appointment.

Surprisingly enough, the reporter found a great deal of support for Edwin Stanton. "But," Thomas pushed one Senator, "Stanton's a Democrat! You think he's the one for the job?"

"Thomas, we're at war now! We need the best man for the job and Stanton is that man. Why, he's one of us!"

Jacob talked to one legislative assistant. "Why would the senators who question General McClellan's abilities want to put a McClellan supporter in the War Department?"

"Jacob, let me tell you a little secret." the man answered. "Edwin Stanton is a lot more interested in Edwin Stanton than he is being anyone's friend. If he gets approved, and I'm betting he will and fast, I believe you will see him dancing to Lincoln's tune, not McClellan's! Mark my words, you will see a different man once he hits the War Department."

"Hmmph!," Thomas harrumphed to Jacob as they made their way through the capital's streets. "Seems to be a case of 'you scratch my back and I'll scratch yours.' Stanton seems to have done a bit of bending in recent days. He must really want this job!"

It was soon clear that not only the Senate was enamored with Stanton. One of Thomas's main competitors, Horace Greeley at the *New York Tribune*, wrote appreciatively of Stanton. He seemed convinced Stanton was the man for the job. "Stanton," he wrote knew how to deal with "the greatest danger now facing the country - treason in Washington, treason in the army itself, especially the treason which wears the garb of unionism."

It turned out the congressmen knew exactly what they were talking about. Stanton was easily confirmed and on the new job within days. And the aide seemed to know what he was about as well. Stanton did appear to be dancing to Lincoln's tune.

At the end of his first day as the new Secretary of War, Thomas' lead article ran with this Stanton statement. "I will force this man McClellan to fight or throw up," the new Secretary promised. "This army has got to fight or run away. While men are striving nobly in the West, the champagne and oysters on the Potomac must be stopped!

Jacob read the quote. "Champagne and oysters, huh? That's a pretty strong quote." He gave Thomas a look. "Sure seems the new secretary is not quite the friend the commanding general thought he was." Thomas could only nod. Things were not as he had thought.

Meanwhile back at the Congress, the attention turned from Edwin Stanton back to General George McClellan

Strangely enough, after leaving his sickbed to attend the White House meeting, McClellan did not return to it. Instead he threw himself back into the training and organizing of the Army of the Potomac. Soon he was seen riding around town inspecting troops and camps.

"Well, that's enough for me!" one senator announced. "If he's well enough to parade around town, he's well enough to appear in front of us!" They ordered the general to appear and testify. McClellan did.

Senators Wade and Chandler did most of the questioning. Why was the army not moving south? McClellan launched into a long-winded lecture on warfare. Disgusted and not receiving the answers they sought, they dismissed the witness. As McClellan left though, Chandler turned to Wade and said, "I don't know much about war, but it seems to me that this is infernal, unmitigated cowardice!" General McClellan thought he had cleverly escaped the committee but really, he was on the edge of big trouble.

The committee decided it had no choice but to return to the president. They arrived at the White House, seething with anger.

"Mr. President," stormed Wade, "you are murdering your country by inches. Mr President, McClellan must be replaced!"

"With whom?" asked the president

"Why with anybody," came the answer.

"Wade, anybody will do for you, but I must have somebody!" the president retorted.

McClellan stayed on his job.

And then stunning news came from the western theatre of the war. The headlines blared "Union Victories!" A new general was suddenly dominating the news - General Ulysses S. Grant. In early February, Grant, with the help of the navy, captured two Confederate forts, Fort Henry and then ten days later Fort Donelson. Suddenly, the North had not one but two victories over the Rebels.

Grant was taking Confederate forts in the West, General George Thomas had forced the Rebels from Eastern Kentucky and General Ambrose Burnside was finding success on the shores of North Carolina. Meanwhile, McClellan sat in Washington. The contrast was striking.

And President Lincoln was paying close attention. He again consulted McClellan who once again assured him the time to move south was not yet right.

Instead of acting against the rebels, McClellan assembled 12 of his division commanders for the president. In an 8-4 vote, they assured Lincoln that the Urbana Plan would be the best, when of course the time was right.

Then, in early March, 1862, the Urbana Plan died. Two events combined to kill it. On March 8, the Confederate ironclad *Virginia* steamed out of the port of Norfolk and instantly changed the naval balance of power around the world. The *Virginia* was an ironclad! It quickly ran through the Union wooden warships decimating them. The *Virginia* first attacked the Union wooden warships, *Congress* and *Cumberland*. The *Congress* unleashed a barrage against the attacking Confederate ship with no result. The cannon balls bounced off the *Virginia's* iron sides. The *Congress* was quickly attacked and the *Cumberland* rammed. Both ships were destroyed. The *Virginia* sailed on seeking other Federal targets.

Two hours after the attack, a telegram reached Washington describing the carnage. Suddenly, Lincoln knew, his cabinet knew, and the citizens of Washington knew. George McClellan also knew that his Urbana Plan was in serious jeopardy. That plan counted on the navy. The navy was to provide transport and flanking protection. McClellan needed to be able to sail untroubled down into the Chesapeake Bay. If this new Confederate vessel controlled the waters, the plan was dead

The second blow to the plan happened almost on the same day. The Rebel forces that McClellan planned to sail around - those forces were gone! Joe Johnson had retreated south from Manassas and was now camped on the Rappahannock River. If McClellan landed today at his previously selected site, he would be landing in the middle of a entrenched Rebel army. Clearly, the Urbana Plan was out.

Thomas shared a rumor that was flying around Washington with Jacob. "Evidently," Thomas declared, "General McClellan's scouts did not discover that the rebels had turned tail. Evidently an escaped slave brought the news in. The army was preparing to attack an empty camp."

Wags around Washington made much of this fact. McClellan couldn't even see an entire army moving? Civilians knew more about the rebel army's movements than the Army of the Potomac did?

The news for McClellan then got worse. When McClellan did send men to inspect the deserted camps, newspaper reporters accompanied them. It wasn't long until the American public was reading about "dangerous Quaker guns, those fake guns made of wooden logs", which had been keeping McClellan at bay. One reporter penned the line "We are utterly dispirited, ashamed, and humiliated." The reporters also announced that based on the size of the camp, the rebels could not have been anywhere as large a force as McClellan had been continually repeating. To many Americans readers, the commanding general seemed to have earned a rather large black eye.

It wasn't just the American people who read these papers. Members of Congress read the newspapers as well. After reading these articles, some Congressmen decided they needed to inspect the deserted rebel works for themselves. They did and McClellan's black eye deepened.

The day they returned from their tour, Radical Republicans introduced a resolution to remove McClellan. It was narrowly defeated but things certainly looked bad for the Little Napoleon.

But then the sun began to shine on the commander of the Army of the Potomac. The vote to remove him had barely failed, but it had failed. He was still commander of the Army of the Potomac. And equally importantly, the threat of the Confederate ironclad was removed. A Federal ironclad, the *Monitor,* had arrived and fought the *Virginia* to a stand still. At least for now, the water route was open again.

McClellan returned to his maps and began planning anew.

McClellan's new plan became known as the Peninsula Campaign. This second plan also called for sailing troops down the Chesapeake, thereby avoiding a land march toward Richmond. This time though, he proposed landing at Fort Monroe and marching up past

Yorktown and Williamsburg, Virginia into Richmond, Virginia.

After finishing his plan, McClellan showed that he had learned from past mistakes. Instead of sharing this plan with Lincoln and Stanton, he chose another path. He called a conference of his generals and announced his plan. "Gentlemen, this is the plan I propose. I'd like to hear your votes; shall we proceed, yea or nay?"

The majority of the generals agreed with their commander and the plan was endorsed. Again, instead of personally sharing with and informing his superiors, General McClellan chose another path. This time he sent a messenger to the White House. General McDowell was dispatched to let the bosses know what McClellan had on tap.

Neither Lincoln nor Stanton liked the plan, but they did not kill it. Instead they created a list of conditions that they handed to General McDowell. These must be met before McClellan could leave the capital. When informed, McClellan readily telegraphed his assent. He then went to work putting together what turned out to be the largest amphibian operation ever attempted in the Americas.

Thomas and Jacob knew nothing about any of this of course. What they did know was that suddenly, no real rumors were caroming around the capital. Thomas could not even get a guess as to what they generals might be planning. Evidently, General McClellan was keeping his cards close to his vest this time.

So the two were very surprised when Thomas received an invitation to visit Lieutenant Colonel Webb at the War Department. The surprise was a pleasant one but it left Thomas wondering what the invitation was all about.

The next day, he quickly found out.

Thomas made his way to the War Department, where he was welcomed to Lieutenant Colonel Webb's office. Taking Thomas' hand enthusiastically, Webb escorted Thomas to a round table. A large map covered the table. Astonishingly then, with barely more than a howdy-do, Lieutenant Colonel Webb set about explaining the new campaign to the reporter.

"You see, Thomas, of course, the instant advantages," Webb said. "We will embark on navy ships from Alexandria." Webb pointed to the Virginia city. "Then protected by the naval escort ships we will make our way down the Potomac and into the Chesapeake." His finger traced the route. "The troops will be safely and quickly moved down into southern Virginia." His finger dropped further south and tapped at a point. "Here, is Fort Monroe. We will disembark there, form, and march our way up this peninsula." His hand swept northwest from the bay. "From the fort to Yorktown, to Williamsburg and on into Richmond. We will defeat the rebels wherever we find them and capture their capital. We will put down this rebellion and end the war!"

Webb turned from the map and looked at Thomas. "And Thomas, my friend, here's the last thing. We'd like to invite you to come along with us. How would you like to be the one that tells the world about our amazing campaign?"

And with that bombshell, Thomas found himself heading back to Virginia.

Chapter 10

The next few weeks were a whirlwind. Jacob was granted permission to accompany Thomas as long as it was understood that he would be staying in Fort Monroe. "No matter where the army might march, Jacob," Thomas strongly admonished, "you are staying at Fort Monroe!"

"Yes, Sir! Yes Sir!!" Jacob instantly promised. Jacob's instant agreement made Thomas nervous.

Thomas spoke to the Dodge House manager about keeping their rooms. "How long will you be gone, Sir?" the manager asked.

Thomas realized he had no idea. It didn't seem like it would be a very long absence. Officers continually and confidently spoke of "a short trip down South." They believed it would be a quick, concentrated campaign. Luckily, the Dodge House owners liked the fact that Thomas put the name of their establishment in his by-line. It now read, "Thomas Henderson, reporting from the Dodge House, Washington, D.C." Arrangements were made.

So it came to be that on March 17, when the first troops sailed out of Alexandria, Virginia, Thomas and Jacob sailed with them. The last thing he did before boarding was to file an article with The *Constitutionalist*. Somehow, Thomas had obtained the text of a telegram that had been sent to the War Department.

The readers of the *Constitutionalist* read: "From the Commanding General to the Secretary of War: Rely upon it that I will carry this thing through handsomely!" The Peninsula Campaign was underway!

After that scoop, the next few days were a bit anti-climatic. Both Thomas and Jacob were pleased to find out that Sergeant Emerson was sailing down with them. He even graciously stepped in to help with some details.

Jacob, unfortunately, spent most of his time being seasick. "Ain't never been on a big ship before," he moaned.

"And you still haven't been on one," returned a non-sympathetic Sergeant Emerson.

Thomas did his best to ferret out some new information for a story, but all he found were enthusiastic officers seemingly full of the exact same information. They all assured him that this was the largest operation of the war. It would be the fastest, it would be the most successful, the war is nearly over, etc. He heard nothing new, nothing worth an article. Thomas could only jot down notes.

A week later, much to Jacob's ever lasting relief, they arrived in southeastern Virginia. The troops began disembarking at Old Point Comfort. Jacob was thrilled to be back on solid ground. True to his word, Sergeant Emerson stopped ribbing Jacob enough to help them find a room. When he saw their accommodations, Thomas became relatively sure Lieutenant Colonel Webb had helped them as well. They were placed in a very nice waterfront home. The owners had no current use of it, Thomas was assured.

Thomas found that he had mixed feelings about being in southeast Virginia. He had first come as a student; now he was part of an invading army. Lieutenant Colonel Webb had taken issue with the term 'invading army', however. Thomas was not part of an invading army, according to Lieutenant Colonel Webb. "Hold right there, Thomas," Webb had admonished him. "We're not invading anything! We are merely United States Soldiers moving within the United States. Same thing has been happening since President Washington's times!"

"But, Sir!" Thomas protested, "Hasn't Virginia left the Union? Isn't it in a state of rebellion?"

"No Thomas, we don't acknowledge that. We do agree that there are residents living within Virginia that are in a state of rebellion, but we do not believe the state of Virginia is in rebellion."

It sounded like legalese to Thomas, but again, his lack of military and legal knowledge stopped him from arguing the point. He decided he needed lawyerly experience to argue with Lieutenant Colonel Webb on this one.

Over the course of the next week the Army of the Potomac arrived, disembarked, and reformed at Fort Monroe. Over 120,000 men, all with supplies and accoutrements turned Fort Monroe into the largest city in Virginia! Ship after ship after ship arrived. Seemingly miles of tents were erected. Warehouses were built, filled, and guarded. Thomas reported it all in his daily reports. He shared it all with his readers.

The only fly in the ointment, at least according to the commanding general, was that the Army of the Potomac was outnumbered. McClellan was positive that his men were outnumbered and he shared that thought with anyone he could. He not only believed they were outnumbered, he assured listeners, his forces were dangerously outnumbered. Making sure he did not rush to a disastrous encounter with an entrenched larger enemy, General McClellan used a week to study the situation. Then on April 4, Thomas reported that the general had sent another telegram to Washington. Evidently, the general had made a decision. His message was simple, "From the commanding General to the Secretary of War: I expect to fight tomorrow."

The telegram proved to have only some elements of truth. The army marched, but it did not fight. McClellan's army began its march up the peninsula toward Richmond, but it became immediately bogged down. Waves of rain seemed to fall endlessly. Roads became muddy morasses. Wagons sunk to their axles. "Less of a road than a mass of mud!" complained one Massachusetts soldier.

"It was 18 miles long and 18 inches deep," complained another.

Their woes continued when it was discovered that the maps they were using were hopeless. Roads that were drawn going north and south turned out to be going north and then east. Roads had been given the wrong names.

Creeks that were supposed to be easily crossed, turned out to be rivers filled with surging waters.

But the army persevered and finally, the men slogged their way up to Yorktown. Yorktown! The final battle site of the Revolution! Many men knew the name, but virtually none had ever thought they would ever see the town.

They soon learned there was no time for sightseeing. Once they reached the town's borders, they ran smack into General McClellan's worst fear. As they watched, they saw Confederate regimental flag after regimental flag march past defended positions. The Rebels were entrenched. Upon evaluation, McClellan's experts announced that based on their information, the Army of the Potomac faced between 150,000 to 200,000 dug in, highly armed, highly motivated Rebel soldiers.

Thomas' article on the first part of the Yorktown campaign carried a quote from General Keyes, "no part of the line, so far discovered, can be taken by assault without an enormous waste of life." Thomas' readers learned that Chief Engineer Brigadier General John G. Barnard called the comprehensive series of redoubts and rifle pits arrayed along the Warwick River "one of the most extensive known to modern times."

McClellan's problems continued to mount. Now that he was not racing up the peninsula, as originally planned, he worried the Confederate warship *Virginia* would steam up and shell his army. He was also upset with the president. Lincoln had promised to send some of

General McDowel's troops down to McClellan. Now, the president was holding those troops back.

Those troops, it turned out, were being held back for two reasons. Number one, Congressmen, unhappy with McClellan's slog through Virginia were beginning to make serious accusations. Some people remembered that McClellan used to work with Jefferson Davis. Other members of Congress, furious at McClellan's lack of action, began accusing McClellan of treason. "He's leaving the capital unprotected so the rebels can attack!" they thundered.

The Secretary of War decided to look into the accusation. He sent a team to find out if the capital was indeed unprotected. The results stunned and enraged the secretary. The report said that McClellan left far less men than he said he would. McClellan had said he was leaving 77,456 ready for duty soldiers to protect the capital. The investigators found out there were really about 29,000. "How did this happen?" Stanton demanded. The men reported that McClellan had made some errors in his arithmetic; he had included troops in his count that had not yet arrived in Washington, (though they were due to arrive someday), and he counted some troops twice. The report did not paint a very attractive picture of the commanding general.

The second reason McDowell was still not with McClellan was Stonewall Jackson. The rebels had suddenly shown a strong interest in increasing their presence in northwest Virginia. Rumors were rampant that Confederate forces, under Stonewall Jackson, the famous general from Bull Run, were moving near Winchester, Virginia. Winchester, as the president was very aware was only 70-some miles away from Washington, D.C. He made the decision to stop McDowell's advance down the Chesapeake. Lincoln decided those troops would be needed to defend the capital.

When a telegram reached McClellan asking for an explanation as to why the capital was under defended, he replied by asking the War Department to send him more men. "I need more men to counter the overwhelming odds I face."

Back in Yorktown, McClellan assessed his current state, shared his views with his officers, and changed plans. Instead of the quick attack planned, the Army of Potomac went into siege mode. After a few days of siege, McClellan wired Lincoln."Don't despair! Do not misunderstand the apparent inaction here. Huge works, almost gigantic, have been erected."

And Thomas could confirm that works had indeed been created. Thomas saw them. Trenches had been dug, roads created, huge field mortars were placed. Sawmills were built and hundreds, if not thousands of trees, were felled. About the only thing the army did not do was fight.

"No, no, no!" Lieutenant Colonel Webb scolded Thomas when Thomas asked about the inaction, "we're not falling into that trap! An entrenched enemy has a 10-1 advantage over an attacking force. Add to that, the fact we are so outnumbered, this must be a very cautious, thought-out effort." Thomas, again with no military background or training, took the officer at his word.

Imagine Thomas's surprise then when he woke on May 4, along with the rest of the army, to find those impressive defenses deserted! Empty! The rebels had completely disappeared! They had retreated during the night. They were now marching back up the peninsula, back toward Richmond. Why were they gone? No one seemed to have an answer.

That news came to Washington when the War Department suddenly received a telegram "Yorktown is ours." The news raced across the capital city. Yorktown is ours! McClellan must have defeated the entrenched rebels! A massive victory! On To Richmond!

What the telegram did not say was that no battle was fought. McClellan neglected to mention that the rebels had retreated without a single shot being fired in their direction.

Given a new hand to play, McClellan went back to the planning table. New orders were issued. The army was to come out of siege mode and change back into pursuit mode. Energized, the men quickly marched 20 miles up the peninsula toward Williamsburg. As they approached the town, Thomas found himself strangely excited and apprehensive. He was excited to see the College of William and Mary again, but he was also concerned about what else he might find.

The army should have been concerned as well. On May 5, believing that Williamsburg was under-defended, if not undefended, General McClellan ordered General Joseph Hooker into the town. McClellan believed the rebels were retreating toward Richmond. If his men faced opposition, it would surely be no more than local militia.

The general was wrong. Instead of militia, General Hooker faced Confederate General James Longstreet and his 30,000 Confederate troops. The first battle of the Peninsula Campaign began.

The Confederates held the advantage in the early part of the battle. Hooker attacked but Longstreet's troops were dug in. Hooker was thrown back, but by mid-afternoon, General Philip Kearny arrived to reinforce Hooker. Soon General Hancock arrived. These additions proved to be the difference and Longstreet had to withdraw. The rebels continued their retreat toward Richmond.

But not all the rebel forces in the country were retreating. Stonewall Jackson's men were still north of Richmond in the Valley. His forces attacked and defeated Union General Banks. Washington, D.C. was seized with panic.

Stanton sent a telegram to 13 governors asking for militia help. "Send all the troops forward that you can immediately. Intelligence from various quarters leaves no doubt that the enemy in great force are advancing on Washington."

But McClellan was quick to reply. He disagreed, assuring Lincoln that the Confederates were only trying to "prevent reinforcements being sent to me. All the information I have from balloons, deserters, prisoners, and contrabands agrees in the statement that the mass of Rebel troops are still in the immediate vicinity of Richmond, ready to defend it." He ended the telegram by asking for more troops.

After the Battle of Williamsburg, McClellan continued the army's advance up the peninsula. Thomas rode with them taking notes every step of the way. One day, Thomas found himself riding with men from the Second Maine and the Ninth Massachusetts. Another day he found himself riding with men from the Twentieth Indiana. He decided to ask if anyone might be from Salem, Indiana.

"No we're Fayette County boys." came one reply.

"We're from Fountain County northwest of there." said another.

"We're from Zionsville, Indiana, Boone County! We're north of there. But Noah Procter, he's from down south somewheres. Noah, Noah, where are ya?"

After a few minutes, Thomas found himself meeting Corporal Procter.

"Nah, I'm not from there I"m next county over- Jefferson. You want to talk with Jesse Kindell over in Company C. He's got a farm near Salem."

A few more minutes of milling around and Thomas was talking with Private Kindell. "Yeah, I live near Salem, 'bout twelve miles outside of town." He paused, scratching his beard. "Truth be told, I'm nearer South Boston than Salem, though."

"Ah, yes," Thomas said, as if he had any idea in the world where South Boston, Indiana, happened to be. "Did you by chance know a family from Salem named Bunten?"

"Couldn't say I did, not know them I mean. If it's the same, a Bunten family did own a general store in town, but I didn't personally-like know them."

"Might you know what became of them?"

Private Kindell scrunched his face up in thought. "Welllll… I seem to recollect…" he paused searching his memory. "Uhmmm, the store closed a while back. In '60, maybe '61? Illness if I remember right. Believe it took the whole family." He looked at Thomas, and asked, "Kin of yours?"

"No, just looking for information. Thanks for your time." Kindell nodded and Thomas rode away. He realized he had his first bit of confirmation about Jacob. Funny, it was the first time he'd really looked into the boy's story. He shook his head. The day they met surely seemed like life times ago. They certainly had come a long way from that first rainy night in that barn.

The next day, Thomas rode with another regiment, this time one from his home state. He rode with the men of the 44th New York. These men wore a Zouave uniform; a dark blue Zouave jacket with red piping on the cuffs, and dark blue trousers with a red stripe. Thomas had to admit, they made quite the appearance. Idly he wondered though, did those colors make you a better target? He chose not to ask the men.

As he rode with the New Yorkers, he happened across an officer he'd previously met, Colonel Arden Freeman. Like Thomas, Freeman was a resident of the Great City of New York. They had conversed a few times over the last few weeks and the two had struck up a friendly relationship.

Thomas called to the man, "Colonel Freeman! How do you fare, Sir?"

Freeman, turned to see Henderson. "Thomas, bully to see you! Bully!"

The two men rode toward each other. As they did, a third horseman came up the road behind them. He began loudly calling to Freeman.

"Please, please, please, Lord above, tell me they are not letting Black Irish from New York City serve as officers in this army!'

Colonel Freeman straightened in the saddle and snapped a salute at the approaching horseman.

"And why, pray tell not?" Colonel Freeman shot back "After all they're letting one armed French New Jersey college boys serve as generals!"

The rider reined in sharply with a broad smile on his face. The two men shook hands warmly.

"Philip, you old soul, how are you?"

"Well, Arden, well." The general replied. "And you?"

"As well as can be expected, given that I'm riding through Virginia instead of being back home in New York."

The general laughed, "Ah, well, you'd just be in trouble back home."

"Trouble is it? Well if that's not the kettle calling the pot black! If anyone knows trouble..."

An amused Thomas watched the exchange.

"Philip," Colonel Freeman said, releasing the general's hand, "allow me to introduce a fellow New Yorker. General Philip Kearny of New York City, meet Thomas Henderson also of New York City."

Thomas extended his hand in welcome. A sharp look crossed Kearny's face.

"Not the Thomas Henderson, surely? Not the reporter for the *Constitutionalist!*"

That comment stopped Thomas in his tracks. "Well, Sir, I do write for the *Constitutionalist*, but I'd be very surprised if you'd heard my name."

Kearny leaned forward, swiftly sticking his hand out to Thomas.

"Not heard your name? Nonsense! I'm an admirer, Sir! Outstanding work, Sir, truly outstanding. The honor is mine."

As Thomas shook the general's hand a strange thought hit him. He realized it was the second time he had come face to face with a reader who just happened to be a general in the Army of the Potomac. The thought made him smile.

Kearny continued. "I've read several of your articles, Sir. They helped me keep abreast of the war."

Puzzled, Thomas said "Sir?"

Freeman laughed, "Thomas this regiment is a mass of fresh fish! Thirty-one days ago, they were all back enjoying Good Old New York! It's only freshly assembled. They may appear to be highfalutin', but they are as green as new corn." He swung around to look at General Phil

Kearny. "Though it is true this old man may have been around the barn once or twice."

"Old Man, is it Adron?! May I remind you we are the same age?"

Freeman gave a hearty laugh, "Touché."

Kearny turned to Thomas, "So you were invited to come down and tour Virginia?"

Colonel Freeman spoke before Thomas could. "Oh, this area is old news to Thomas, Philip. This is his home away from home. He attended The College of William and Mary in Williamsburg."

"Williamsburg!? I'm sure you had a much different experience there than I did!"

"Yes Sir, I heard about that battle." Thomas responded. "That will be my next article."

Kearny responded forcefully, "Well don't talk to those buffoons at Fort Monroe! They act like they don't even know Hooker and I were there!"

"Ah, yes,"Thomas said, searching for a diplomatic answer "I did read General McClellan's dispatches."

Kearny fairly exploded, "Fiction, Sir,", he spat. "Purely nothing but fiction!"

Seeking to move away from this potentially explosive subject, Colonel Freeman turned back to Thomas. "Philip spent his college days in our native city. We both attended Columbia."

"Columbia!" Thomas said. "That's where my family wanted me to go."

Kearny gave a snorted laugh. "Strangely enough that's what my family wanted, as well. The difference is they ended up getting what they wanted. I wanted to go to West Point, but they were adamantly opposed!"

"I barely escaped a similar fate." Thomas admitted. "They wanted me to enter medicine, I wanted anything else. I was able to talk them into William and Mary, or it would have been Columbia for me for sure." He quicky looked at both men. "No offense, of course!"

The two laughed. "None taken!"

The three men continued to talk as they followed the column of marching troops. It turned out Freedman had practiced law after graduation. Kearny had inherited money from his grandfather, said goodbye to the law and entered the military. They continued talking as they rode the muddy Virginia roads. Despite the age difference, Thomas fit in quite nicely with the two friends.

Eventually the conversation turned to their current situation. "So Philip, what can we expect up the road?" Freeman asked, nodding in the general direction of Richmond.

"From what I hear Arden there's not much opposition. And we're giving them every chance to get away from us, aren't we? We certainly are taking our own sweet time getting there! I wouldn't be surprised if the war is over before the Virginia Creeper moves us up the road!"

"Philip!" a shocked Freeman warned.

Kearny waved the warning away, "Oh, Arden, we're all friends here. And believe me, I'm not telling Mr. Henderson anything he doesn't already know. He is a newspaper man after all! He's been around!"

Thomas tried to look nonplused, but Kearny's response surprised him. To hear a general in the army insult the commander! To hear him express such outright insubordination!

But he had to admit, there had been a tingling when he heard the phrase "Virginia Creeper." He had become increasingly uncomfortable with how slowly the advance had happened. All that talk about, "We fight tomorrow; victory is ours. We will race up the Peninsula!", turned out only to be empty talk. Yorktown was supposed to be a siege, the Rebels left. Williamsburg was supposed to be under-defended and it became a full blown battle a battle the North quite easily could have lost. The Army of the Potomac had been in Virginia for almost six weeks. What did they have to show for their efforts? The situation had given Thomas a lot to think about.

In the end, Kearny was right about the opposition. The Army of the Potomac made its way to the outskirts of Richmond, almost unopposed. But the easy march? Well, not so much. The rains, and the mud they produced, never seemed to never stop. Mud was everywhere. In the three weeks following the battle of Williamsburg, most men had not marched more than 50 miles, total. No quick march here.

When asked why the quick march didn't happen, Thomas was generally given the same few reasons.

"Well the gunboats have sailed up the James", (as if that were the answer to why the troops weren't marching), "and of course, the horrible weather, the horrible roads" and the answer he was beginning to hear over and over again, "and of course we must move cautiously, being so badly outnumbered here in enemy territory."

And move cautiously they did. The army slowly, very slowly, made it's way up the Pamunkey River. They created supply posts along the way, at places like Eltham's Landing, Cumberland Landing and White House Landing. Each stop was a bit closer to the outskirts of Richmond.

Meanwhile the Rebels had fallen into a defensive position between the Chickahominy River and the northeast edge of Richmond. As the Union soldiers made camp between the Pamunkey and the Chickahominy rivers, they could hear the church bells of Richmond chime.

Meanwhile, the Chickahominy itself became another obstacle for the Union. During dry weather, the river was narrow, and crossing was easy, but May of 1862 was not a dry time. The incessant rain brought the Chickahominy to flood stage. It turned into a virtual morass, extending in some places nearly a mile across.

For a week, little changed in either army. McClellan did send Stanton a telegraph saying, "We will soon be at them and I am sure of the result." When he read that telegram, President Lincoln said "And I am becoming sure these telegraphs mean nothing. When will they fight? When will he act?"

Lincoln telegraphed McClellan back. "Can you get near enough to throw shells into the city?" he asked. He followed that with a second telegraph. "I think the time is near when you must either attack Richmond or else give up the job and come to the defense of Washington." McClellan telegraphed back another request for reinforcements.

Pickets exchanged shots and there were numerous skirmishes but pickets also exchanged newspapers and traded coffee for tobacco. One day, Thomas rode to the front lines. He gazed across a meadow to see a dozen rebels brazenly picking berries under the bright Virginia sun.

Thomas used the quiet time to do a bit of research. He also worked to cultivate a source. General Phil Kearny of New York captivated him. How did he lose his arm? Why was he so dismissive of General McClellan? What was his story? Thomas began to dig asking questions when he could.

He found out that Kearny was born into wealth in New York City. He had wanted to join the military, but his family insisted on Columbia. In 1836, his grandfather died, leaving Kearny a fortune of over $1 million. He then chose to join the military. Strangely enough, he had served with Jefferson Davis of Mississippi on the western frontier. But then as Thomas was learning, most officers had friends on both sides.

Then the Mexican War broke out. Kearny was highly praised for his efforts in that war. He also lost his arm. After the war, Thomas learned, Kearny had gone to France to fight as a soldier of fortune. He returned to the States and when the war broke out, he offered his services to the North.

He was known as a bit irascible. He had the reputation of being downright disrespectful to those he disagreed with, be they above him or below him in rank. He was also known to be devoted to friends and family. Thomas had seen that side of the general. Thomas found him interesting, charming, and most importantly forthright. He decided to write Kearny and ask for an appointment.

Evidently Kearny was interested in Thomas as well, because Thomas received a quick reply. He invited Thomas to accompany him on an informal inspection of the troops. Thomas instantly accepted.

Two days later, the men met. After initial greetings, Kearny jumped right to it. "Fine article on the Williamsburg battle!" he complimented Thomas.

"Thank you, Sir, I took your advice and cultivated multiple sources." Following Kearny's lead, Thomas jumped to it as well."Sir, if I may, there's a rumor running - well, let me just ask you - for the record - did you really ride into battle at Williamsburg yelling, "I'm a one-armed Jersey son-of-a-gun, follow me!"

The general laughed. "Well, that's what my men tell me I did."

Thomas shook his head in disbelief. "Did you really yell, "Don't worry, men, they'll all be firing at me!?"

Kearny laughed again.

"And is it true," Thomas continued, "that at one point, you led the charge with your sword in hand, and your reins in your teeth?"

Kearny smiled and said, "I learned to ride with the reins in my teeth in France."

During the course of the afternoon's ride, Thomas learned a great deal about the general and his opinions. He learned, as he had surmised from the Virginia Creeper comment, that Kearny was frustrated by McClellan's lack of aggressiveness. He also learned that Kearny had a high opinion of his own abilities. "I can do a better job at division, corps, or even army level than any man now holding higher rank than mine," he said.

Thomas thoroughly enjoyed the day, but he left not knowing exactly how much he should write about General Kearny. He didn't have the chance to give that subject much additional thought however because on May 31st, the rebels got everyone's attention. They surprised almost everyone in the Army of the Potomac by suddenly switching from defense to offense. The rebels attacked the Army of the Potomac.

After weeks of inaction, General Johnson's rebels came storming out of their camps and attacked McClellan on multiple fronts. Over the next two days the battle raged. Ultimately, the Rebels were unable to drive the Army of the Potomac away. The Yankees were able to hold on to their position but only after suffering approximately 5,000 casualties.

The day of the battle found Thomas in a state. He had spent the previous day at McClellan's headquarters attempting to get information for a story. He had gotten very little information. He went to bed frustrated that he had wasted the day.

Then, the next morning, he heard the gunfire. He attempted to ride to the action but had been denied permission. He had been forbidden to move. He sat at H.Q. stewing. His mood continued to get darker. As he sat, he vowed right then and there that no one would detain him again! "Thomas Henderson is not going to miss any more important stories!" he promised.

At the end of the battle, there was some news. Thomas reported that one of the most important casualties was on the rebel side. General Joseph Johnson had been struck by a piece of shrapnel and forced to leave the field. Thomas read about the incident in a Richmond newspaper and promptly shared it with his readers. He was glad for the information but it had always baffled him that Richmond newspapers made their way so frequently into the northern camps. In those papers, Thomas read that Jefferson Davis had placed a man named Robert E. Lee in command. "Robert E. Lee?" Thomas thought to himself, "Now where have I heard that name before?"

General McClellan had heard the name. McClellan told his staff he was pleased with the change. Johnston was a fighter, he said, " I prefer Lee to Johnson! Lee will be cautious..weak...wanting in moral firmness...likely to be timid and irresolute in action."

The General then went on to claim complete victory in the battle he called the Battle of Fair Oaks, "It is a complete Union victory," he declared.

But strangely enough though, after achieving that complete victory, McClellan did not press on. Instead of attacking, he went into siege mode. He was going to lay siege to the city of Richmond. For the next three weeks his army did not advance an inch. His army seemed to go into hiatus.

And then Robert E. Lee struck.

Actually, to be truthful, as Thomas wrote, McClellan delivered the first strike. After his three-week wait, McClellan suddenly felt compelled to move. There were two apparent reasons, though the general never acknowledged either one. Thomas believed those reasons were Jeb Stuart and Stonewall Jackson.

General McClellan at first, then later and consistently ever after said, "It was of no military consequence," but Thomas was absolutely stunned to learn that Confederate General Jeb Stuart had led his calvary troops on a jaunt around, AROUND, the entire Army of the Potomac! Thomas was not the only one amazed. People across the country sat up and took notice.

At approximately 2 a.m., on June 12, Stuart had ridden to his commanders and simply said, "Gentlemen, in ten minutes everyone must be in the saddle." Those words put a thousand rebel riders into motion. They left Richmond, rode northwest toward Stonewall Jackson's position, and then suddenly cut back to the east. They then proceeded to ride completely around the northern troops.

Thomas was aghast. McClellan may have dismissed it, but it caught the full attention of the army, the president, the press and the country. They were all astonished at the deed.

Thomas believed that Stonewall Jackson's rumored actions was the second reason McClellan moved. Fresh off his victories in the Valley, Stonewall was said to be heading south to join Lee. McClellan certainly did not want Lee to receive any more troops, firmly believing he was outnumbered as it was.

So Little Mac decided to move before Jackson could arrive. He decided to move his siege artillery a mile closer to Richmond. To accomplish this he decided he needed to occupy a place called Oak Grove. Accordingly, the attack was ordered.

The attack did not succeed. The Yankees found themselves bogged down in a swamp and Confederate Benjamin Huger's men were able to counter attack. In an odd twist, a southern regiment wearing red Zouave uniforms attacked a New York regiment wearing red Zouave. The New Yorkers held their fire as the rebels approached, assuming, based on their uniforms, that the approaching troops were Union. When their commander realized that no Union troops would be coming from the direction of Richmond, the New York boys opened fire. The Confederates took the day.

General McClellan was not at the battle. He was three miles to the rear. He did however, send a telegram ordering his men to withdraw. He then sent a second telegram announcing that he would be arriving to take command. Two and a half hours passed as the Union troops waited for his arrival. By the time the general arrived one thousand men on both sides had fallen. No further Union action was ordered. No ground had been gained by the Army of the Potomac.

Robert E. Lee however had learned what he needed to know. He decided to rearrange the chess board. The next day, Southern troops attacked the Union forces. With this attack, General Lee changed the entire tenor of the Peninsula Campaign and of the war.

Chapter 11

Thomas woke from a deep, medicated sleep. He floated toward the surface. His eyes flitted and the room instantly started spinning. "Ugghhh..." he muttered.

"Lie still, Sir, lie still. You are going to be fine." Just hearing the words hurt Thomas' head. He decided to drop back into darkness.

Thomas woke from a deep, medicated sleep. He floated toward the surface. As he opened his eyes the room started to spin.

"Stay still Thomas, stay still." The voice was familiar, but Thomas could not name the speaker. He felt a gentle patting on his arm.

He decided to close his eyes again, That stopped the room from spinning. He continued to listen though. "Uggghh." he struggled.

"Stay still, Thomas," came the voice "you're going to be fine and you're in a safe place."

"And you're a VIP!!" came another voice. This time he recognized the voice. The face floated up to him. "Mmmm," he tried again. "Jacob?" he croaked.

"Yes, Sir!"

"Good, good..." and Thomas drifted down again.

"And I'm a VIP!" Jacob proudly announced, but Thomas had already drifted back.

Sergeant Emerson looked down at the boy. "VIP?"

"Certainly, Sir! I've had a general of the Army of the Potomac call on me! Where I come from, that makes you a VIP!"

"Hmmpphh!" Sergeant Emerson snorted, knowing exactly how that visit came about. He ruffled the boy's hair and left the room.

Thomas woke from a deep, medicated sleep. He floated toward the surface. As he opened his eyes the room started to spin.

"Stay still Thomas, stay still." The voice was not familiar but it was comforting. Thomas blinked his eyes and the room slowly, slowly started to come to rest.

"Relax, Thomas." the deep voice continued. "You're going to be fine; you're under a doctor's care. You're going to be fine." The voice was calm and reassuring. "You were wounded but you are going to be fine."

"Wounded?" Thomas croaked

"Yeup," came Jacob's familiar voice. "Rebel cannonball."

Panic instantly seized him. Thomas' hands began racing over his body searching for injuries.

"Does that every time doesn't he?" Jacob chortled.

"Not really kind or very comforting, Jacob." Sergaent Emerson admonished. "Thomas you are fine. You were not hit with a cannonball, you were standing nearby when one exploded. You are concussed but will be 100% fine."

Thomas reacted with a deep sigh. His hands dropped back to his side. Perhaps,… he knew part of this? Slowly bits and pieces began coming back to him. He was, maybe had been, in a hospital… in Virginia? He had been with the army at…everything seemed to swirl in fog.

"Don't worry about remembering," the doctor said, as if he could read Thomas' mind. "It will all come back in due time. You're concussed. You will be fine."

"You were knocked into a cocked hat!" Jacob announced proudly.

"Whaaaaa….?"

It took another day or so before Thomas was able to truly focus. Once he could, he pestered everyone for news. What in the world had happened to him? What had happened to the army?

The first part of the story was provided by another newsman, Charles Page of the *New York Tribune*. Charles had also been traveling with the army during the Peninsula Campaign.

"So, Charles, tell me…what happened to me? What happened to the Army? How in the world did I get back to Fort Monroe?"

"It's a long story; there's much to tell." Charles started. "Evidentally, crazily enough, you took it in your head to travel to a battle."

Sergeant Emerson, who was also visiting, said in a disapproving voice "And I thought you'd learned better than that at Bull Run!"

"I remember that!" Thomas said excitedly. "I missed the Seven Pines and Oak Grove. I was determined to see what was happening. I had to find out what was going on!"

"What's the last thing you remember?" Charles asked.

"Let's see. I remember riding up the road toward Mechanicsville. I joined up with John Reynold's men. We were near Beaver Dam Creek, and I could see the rebels coming from the west. They were just starting to form. Reynolds had ordered the men up and..." He stopped. A puzzled look came over him. "And that's the last thing I remember."

Charles nodded. "You were standing with a group of officers when A. P. Hill's artillery opened up. Evidently you were close to a cannonball when it exploded. As you know, you weren't wounded, but you were concussed. Evidently you dropped like a rock and to the men standing around you, for all the world, you looked dead!"

Sergeant Emerson continued the tale. "Luckily," he said wryly, "officers draw surgeons. One examined you and determined you were probably concussed but not dead. Or at least you hadn't died yet."

Charles leaned in and in a very serious voice said, "We're lucky to have you with us, Thomas."

He continued. "Evidently, you were placed in an ambulance and taken to Harrison's Landing. I think you were lucky to be asleep for that trip." Army ambulances were notorius for being unpleasant rides. Hot canvas top, iron ringed wheels banging over nasty roads. Summer

Virginia heat, lying next to wounded soldiers. It would have been a long 40-mile trip. "Once there you were placed in the hospital."

"And then, Thomas, you were lucky enough to have General Kearny take an interest in you. He sent an aide back to see how you were doing."

"The aide reported back that you would probably live though that was not certain. Kearny asked if you were improving in the hospital and it turned out nothing more could be done for you there. Time, it turned out would be the key."

"Well if that's the case," Kearny said, "lets move him back to Fort Monroe."

Kearny arranged a private carriage to transport Thomas. It was incredibly generous but it was still a 60-mile trip. Thomas did remember parts of this painful ride. When the carriage hit bumps in the destroyed roads, Thomas felt waves of pain and fireworks exploded in his head. It was a tough ride.

Thomas, it turned out, had been basically unconscious from June 28 to July 2. The doctors at Fort Monroe agreed with their counterparts at Harrison's Landing and believed Thomas was going to be fine - probably. Either way there was nothing they could do. So General Kearny checked Thomas out of the Fort Monroe hospital and returned him to the Newkirk house.

"And that's where I found you" said Sergeant Emerson. "After Malvern Hill we were in the retreat with everyone else...",

"Hold on there, Sergeant Emerson!" Charles interrupted, "Retreat? Don't you mean the redeployment to our change of base?"

Emerson gave him a wry smile. "Anyway, we ended up here. And I stopped by the house on the chance you were here. You were, of course, but you were in a pickle. I have to say you did not look good, Thomas."

"Thank you," Thomas responded.

"But the doctors kept insisting you were going to be alright," pushed in Jacob. "Even when I didn't believe them."

One day a surgeon had stopped by to examine Thomas. Jacob stopped the surgeon as he was leaving the house. "He's going to live, isn't he?" Jacob worriedly asked.

"Well usually if a patient is going to die, they would have done it by now."

"But he hasn't said a thing in four days!" protested Jacob.

"And that's also very normal." the doctor said, but he also offered the quip "or not" in a low mutter. Jacob had not been reassured.

"Got to be honest, thought you may not make it." Jacob said.

"Touch and go!" agreed Charles.

"But I was fine, I am fine so let's not dwell on that!" Thomas said, "All's well and all that stuff and nonsense! So tell me, what happened to the army after I was wounded?"

"Oh, Thomas. It is a strange, sad tale."

"How so?"

"Are you sure you're ready for all this?"

"Yes," Thomas assured them, "I need to know."

"Well the Army of the Potomac basically fought a series of six battles. We held our own in five of them and won a clear outright victory in the other. Yet after every battle we retreated, giving way to the rebels."

Thomas was incredulous. "Why in the world would we retreat if we weren't losing? That makes no sense to anyone." He looked over at Jacob. "I don't care if a person was knocked into a cocked hat or not. It It doesn't make sense."

Jacob gave him a grin.

"Ah," said Charles "to get an answer to that question, you'll have to talk to the commanding officer himself. McClellan ordered all the retreats."

Jacob chimed in. "Wouldn't do you any good to talk with McClellan. To hear him tell it, we didn't retreat once. We merely changed our base of operation to better preserve the army." Jacob's tone held an edge of anger.

"It often wasn't pretty," offered Charles. "The retreat looked much like what I imagined Napoleon's retreat from Moscow must have looked like."

"But none of what you are saying makes sense!" Thomas insisted again. "Charles, lay it out for me, step by step."

"Well simply put, as I said, we fought a series of six battles in basically a week. Oak Grove was the first, and Mechanicsville, your high water mark was the second.

Gaines Mill, Garnett's Farm, Savage Station, and Malvern Hill all followed."

"The pattern started after Mechanicsville, although some say it really started after Oak Grove. Rather than attack Richmond after the victory at Mechanicsville, or the draw if you prefer, McClellan surprised us all by deciding that he needed to retreat. "An attack on Richmond,' he announced, 'would be detrimental to the army.' How did he put it to his commanders, oh yes, 'I vow to save this army by retreating to the James River.' "

"But that was the last time we heard the word retreat," Jacob interjected. "Ever since it's been not a retreat but a change of base!"

"Over the next week the pattern stayed the same." Charles resumed. "Lee attacked; we held, then retreated. Lee attacked; we held and then retreated. The only real difference was Malvern Hill. We didn't hold there; we gave the rebels a good whipping."

"But," Jacob jumped in, "we started retreating as soon as we'd won. Maybe even before!"

"True," said Charles, "My interviews show McClellan ordered the tents struck and the wagons packed even before he knew the outcome of the battle."

Thomas could only shake his head in disbelief. To have come so far and accomplished so little. There truly was a great deal to think about.

The next day Thomas had improved enough that he was sitting on the front porch enjoying the sunshine. He was supping on a cup of broth watching the ships on the water when he heard the gate creak open. Turning to the sound, Thomas was very pleasantly surprised to see General Philip Kearny striding toward him. "General Kearny, Goodness! Come up, Sir!"

Climbing up onto the porch, the general swept off his hat. "How are you faring Thomas? You certainly look a lot better than you did the last time I saw you!"

"And I understand I owe that recovery to you, Sir. I cannot possibly thank you enough for your kind care and consideration!"

"Nonsense, glad to do it. New Yorkers have to stick together in these dangerous times." His eyes twinkled as he spoke. "So are you on the mend? How are you?"

"Much, much better, Sir. Again, thanks to you."

"Now, no more of that Thomas! May we put that topic to rest please? If you're able, I've come to talk of other things."

"As you wish, Sir, and I am able. But where are my manners? Please, Sir, at your leisure!"

The general sat in the offered chair, but he did not relax. He began to almost nervously move his hat around in his hand. "I don't really know how to start, I don't really know if it is even appropriate..." his words drifted away and he gazed out toward the sun on the water. Then he shook his head as if to clear it.

"But I've made my decision and you will do with it as you will!" He leaned forward and gazed intently at Thomas. "I don't know how much longer I will be here at Fort Monroe. I'm receiving new orders and I will be glad to get them. But as I began getting ready to head north, I found that I could not leave until I'd talked with you." He paused, took a deep breath and plunged on.

"You see, Thomas, I have come to think of you as a new friend, not just a reporter, and I'm not sure I should put a new friend in this position. But on the other hand, I dare not take any opportunity to do what's right. And you are a respected reporter."

Thomas gave an encouraging nod but he was totally lost.

"Right then, well, let me start. Tell me, Thomas, have you heard that we fought in six engagements, and we broke even or won them all? But after each action, the Army of the Potomac retreated. We just walked away, leaving the field to the smaller army, the army we'd just defeated. Why did we do that?"

"I know you heard me call McClellan the Virginia Creeper. It's true that I think he is too slow, too cautious. I told my wife we were advancing like timid trespassers, not fierce invaders. I told her the hour calls for audacity; we offered timorousness." Kearny paused for a moment, shaking his head sadly before continuing.

"And why was McClellan so often absent from the battlefied? When my men were engaged, I was there. So was Hooker and so was Reynolds. Not McClellan. Why was he absent, attempting to lead his army by telegraph? Why did he sit on a warship on the James while his men were dying on the field? Why was he not on the field when the battle was being fought?"

"You know, Thomas, that in June, we were so close to Richmond that we could hear their church bells chime.

At that time, I wrote my wife that 'If only the Young Napoleon gathered his nerve and loosed one tremendous blow ... I can promise that we would take Richmond at our ease.' And then when McClellan finally decided the time was ripe to make his move, he allowed us, Hooker and me, I mean, to start a limited attack. I was so excited that I rode in front of Robinson's men and promised them 'This is the hour for which we have been longing!' And the men proved I was right. One yelled back, 'We'll see you in Richmond, General Phil!' Thomas, the men were ready! But their commanding general was not. Before we could even fully engage the army, McClellan decided not to push the issue and we ending up doing nothing more than skirmishing!"

"I believe it was that retreat that finally pushed me over the edge. When McClellan said we were leaving the field, I was astonished. 'You mean we retreat?' I asked him. 'Retreat from a smaller enemy force?' He told me it was not a retreat but a change in the base of operations." Kearny paused turning to fully look at Thomas.

"Thomas, I realize we haven't known each other that long, and you may not know this, but I have to admit, I do seem to have a bit of a temper. I threw my hat on a table and flatly told McClellan that his retreat was prompted by cowardice or treason."

Thomas reacted with a small chuckle, "Well, I might have heard a bit about that." He reached for a notebook. "Wait a minute, I want to make sure I get this right." He flipped a few pages and then read, 'Phil unloosed a broadside. He pitched into McClellan with language so strong that all who heard it expected he would be placed under arrest until a general court-martial could be held. I was certain Kearny would be relieved of his command on the spot.'"

Kearny laughed, "Oh my, who'd you convince to talk out of school? No," he said, holding up his hand, "never mind, it's accurate enough."

Thomas shrugged, "I never share my sources."

"Well, you got a good one there. Looking back, it probably was a miracle I was not relieved. But as you can clearly see, I was not listened to either. And our commanding general made his opinion of me quite clear when he placed me in the rear. We were placed so far in the rear, we couldn't even find the front, had we been allowed to look!"

"And that's when I knew I had to leave the Army of the Potomac. That same day I wrote Stanton asking, no begging, for a transfer. I'd had it with McClellan, I asked to be re-assigned to the Army of Virginia."

"And now, Thomas, the re-assignment has been approved. Soon I'll be heading up north to join John Pope. But before I go, I had to share my thoughts with someone, someone who could tell the truth to the people about what's going on. The country needs to know what kind of man is in charge of its army. They should know the war will never be won as long as he is in command."

"Now Thomas, I know you may not be comfortable with this, it is my opinion and I am but one man. But I know in my heart of hearts, I am right. And I know this story needs to be told!"

Kearny took a breath and continued. "You may not be the one to tell the story. You may not agree. You may not think this is a story worth telling. I respect that. But after much thought, believe me, much thought, I decided I had to share it with you." Kearny stopped and took a great breath. "Sorry if I put you in a tough spot," he said.

Thomas shook his head, "Not a tough spot, General, but you've certainly given me a lot to think about. And I have to admit, I was wondering about a few of those things myself."

"I don't expect an instant answer," Kearny answered "but if you think it's worth considering…"

"Indeed it is, Sir and I promise I will!"

"That's all I can ask then." Kearny looked a bit relieved, like a load had been lifted, a chore completed. His hat was dropped on a nearby table. "So what will you do next? Stay here? Head back home?"

Thomas had been thinking about this. "I think I may have learned all I can on this trip. It's time to head back north. Now it's a matter of figuring out how."

"Well, I believe I can help with that task."

And he was as good as his word. The very next day Thomas and Jacob received confirmation of their passage back up the Potomac on a returning troop ship.

Unfortunately it turned out to be another unpleasant voyage. This time Thomas was the one to suffer. The doctor told him it was a case of summer influenza. He assured Thomas it was only a matter of time before he was better. Thomas was convinced the man was an insane liar. For Thomas the entire trip was an endless torment of vomit, diahrea, body aches and massive headaches. He felt as if he were on death's doorstep. This was much worse than the concussion. Both the voyage and his illness seemed neverending.

Finally they arrived back at Alexandria some three and a half months after they'd left to start the campaign. The two stumbled back to the Dodge House and promptly collapsed into their beds.

The next day, Thomas insisted on writing an article for the *Constitutionalist*. Jacob strongly protested, "Mr. Henderson, you are not well! You've not recovered from your illness!"

"That is true, but I must get to work."

"But!.." and then Jacob bit off his words. What he was not quite willing to say was that Thomas was not going to be producing his best work. And Jacob was right. Thomas' subsequent offering was one of his worst stories since that first Battle of Bull Run attempt. Thomas did not see it that way and insisted it be sent north. Jacob would not disobey, but he did take an unprecedented step. He sent the story with an addition, an addition to the editor explaining that Thomas had been wounded but would be back to full form soon.

Thomas sent a second telegraph as well. This one went to his parents. He assured them all was well. He apologized for being out of touch, and he promised a long letter would be coming their way soon.

Both men were astonished by what happened next. A tiny little abridged version of Thomas' article appeared next to a much larger article headlined, " *Famous War*

Correspondent Wounded During Peninsula Campaign."
"Thomas Henderson, star reporter for the *Constitutionalist"*
the article read "was wounded recently as he was
attempting to bring the latest news to our readers. A
cannonball hit the reporter who was lucky to escape with
his life..."

Thomas was aghast. He couldn't find the words.
Finally, he turned to Jacob, "Oh, Jacob what have you
done?"

"Only trying to help sir." Jacob was contrite for one
of the few times in his life and Thomas had to forgive him.
However he also knew he had to send another telegraph
home, Now! He'd not said a word about his condition with
his family, but it appeared he would need to be a little
more forthright now. He sent the telegraph.

Thomas then followed the doctor's advice and
spent a few days taking it easy. His strength gradually
returned and soon Thomas was nearly back to his old self.
He had used the few days off to strongly consider his
position. He had seen Bull Run and he knew first hand
how far the Army of the Potomac had come. He had after
all, written article after article praising General George B.
McClellan for creating the current army of the Potomac.
He had been part of the grand campaign and grand
promise as the army sailed south. But he had also seen that
army, well to be honest, he had seen it misused. He had
come to believe that General Kearny was basically correct.

As he told Jacob, "Oh, I'm sure General Kearny can
go off half cocked, but I am also sure the General knows

what he was talking about!" Thomas decided his next articles needed to reflect that opinion.

Over the next few days Thomas wrote a series of articles that outlined the fiasco that was the Peninsula Campaign. He took the information General Kearny provided and added his own evaluations and observations. Overall, he concluded, the campaign had been a failure. And it was also his conclusion that most of the fault lay directly with one man, the commanding general.

Publisher Comstock approved of this work and again, Thomas' work appeared over a number of days. The articles made a huge splash in New York. Then for the first time his articles were republished in D.C. papers. Soon the citizens of that city and the soldiers in the Army of the Potomac could read his accounts. Then, everywhere he went it seemed, people were talking about the articles. Some were in favor, some were mad as swarming hornets. Few people had no opinion.

As Thomas analyzed the response to his articles and to the other pieces being written, he thought he saw a pattern. On the whole Lincoln supporters, abolitionists, and Republicans were up in arms over General McClellan's decisions and actions. The general was defended by Democrats, pro-unification folks, and anti-abolitionists. "Strange," Thomas thought, "does that make me then a Republican? Or an abolitionist?" He had truly never thought about it. He hadn't even voted in the election of 1860. Strange how time changes you. "All in all though," he thought "I must be in a pretty good place."

Some were happy with his work, some were mad. "Must be doing something right," he concluded.

Chapter 12

One night Thomas returned to the Dodge House to find an ordinary, every day, envelope in his mail. Only when he read the return address "Senator Benjamin Franklin Wade of Ohio," was he hit with a mix of excitement and dread. He ripped the envelope open.

"Dear Mr. Henderson, I wonder if you would do me the courtesy of meeting with two of my associates. If you are agreeable, they will come to your residence at 7p.m. Tuesday evening. Respectfully, Senator Benjamin Franklin Wade."

"Well, Thomas, you've plunged into it now," he admonished himself. He really did not want anything to do with the committee, but one did not dismiss Senator Wade lightly. He had no idea what they wanted, so there was no way to prepare. "Just let the chips fall where they will", he supposed, shrugging.

At the appointed hour, two men knocked on Thomas' Dodge House door. "Good Evening, Mr. Henderson. Thank you for seeing us. I'm Agnus McTeague, and this is Jonathan Rodes." Both men gave Thomas a little bow. "May we come in?"

Thomas invited them in and the three men sat at his table. Jacob sat at the small table in the corner, listening. Thomas introduced him and then offered the men refreshment.

"May I come to the point?" said Mr. McTeague, declining his offer. "We think you might just be the man we are looking for."

Thomas did not react, but that comment chilled him.

Mr. Rodes spoke, "We work for Senator Wade and to be blunt, Sir, it is our opinion, and the senator's, that General McClellan is a traitor. We are on a mission to expose him, and we seek your help with that mission."

And there it was, right out in the middle sitting on the table for all to see.

"Ah," said Thomas noncommittally.

"We know your early work, and we know the admiration you had for the general." said McTeague.

"And we share your appreciation of his work to transform the Army of the Potomac." said Rodes.

McTeague said, "The Army of the Potomac was changed from the mob that attacked Bull Run to a splendid professional army, fully equipped and fully manned."

"But what he has done with that splendid army since it was created is criminal, Sir," Rodes said "and we think you might share our opinion. May we share our information with you and get your evaluation?"

Thomas nodded, "Please do."

McTeague said, "We think that General McClellan took an army that outnumbered his opponent, often 2-1, perhaps even 3-1, yet consistently refused to use that army to destroy his smaller foe. We know for instance that at Yorktown, McClellan's 100,000 men were faced by 15,000, and the 15,000 held him at bay.

"And held him at bay with theatrics, Sir." Rodes jumped in. "We understand they were duped by an amateur thespian! The Rebels are bragging that their General Magruder marched the same men past General McClellan hour after hour while the general sat immobile counting their flags."

"Oh, he took the bait, Sir. He swallowed it hook, line, and sinker. On April 7, he telegraphed, 'All the prisoners state that General J. E. Johnston arrived in Yorktown with strong reinforcements. It seems clear that I shall have the whole force of the enemy on my hands, probably not less than 100,000 men and possibly more.' "

"Our evidence showed he faced no more than 15,000, Sir, 15,000!" Thomas was surprised that they had such information (and he was envious). Where did they get it?

"We know that General McClellan faced the Rebels in battle some six times, drew a draw or victory in each one and after each encounter, retreated as soon as he could!"

Thomas took a breath and then asked "Some of this I have heard, but much of it was in the way of rumor and innuendo. I fear Gentlemen, that I must deal in facts."

Before he could go any further, McTeague jumped in, "Our evidence, Sir." He snapped open a case and pulled out a sheaf of papers. They looked to Thomas like a combination of letters and telegrams. McTeague shook some documents in the air. "Telegrams sent by McClellan himself. If I may…" he pulled on a pair of reading glasses from his vest pocket. As he did, Thomas wondered, "And how did you get those telegrams?" but he dared not wonder outloud.

"First of all, we now believe McClellan did not want to engage at all." He reached for a telegram. "Before any fighting had begun, he sent this series of telegrams to the War Department."

"First the general wrote, "I shall be in perfect readiness to move froward and take Richmond the moment McCall reaches here and the ground will admit the passage of artillery."

"But when McCall reached McClellan", Rodes said "McClellan sent a second telegram. 'I shall attack as soon as the weather and the ground will permit.' Then on June 18, when the weather had improved, he telegrammed, 'After tomorrow we shall fight the rebel army as soon as Providence will permit.' Yet he sat, unmoving as a rock during this whole three week period. He never engaged the enemy once!"

"We're assuming," McTeague said dryly, "that Providence never permitted." He pushed on. "When the fighting did begin, McClellan claimed every that 'victory' was due to his amazing skill."

"But," Rodes jumped in, "he made it clear that any, *any* errors were someone else's fault. Did you know that even before the first shot of the Seven Days Battle, as I understand we are calling it now, McClellan sent this telegram to Secretary Stanton?

'I shall have to contend against vastly superior odds. The Rebels have perhaps 200,000 men. If I am not reinforced, the responsibility cannot be thrown on my shoulders. It must rest where it belongs.' "

"And after he lost Gaines Mill, did you know he sent Stanton yet another telegram?"

"Yes," Thomas said, "I am aware of that." It had become a rather famous telegram.

"I doubt you are aware of the last two sentences. They were never delivered! On June 28 as he began yet another retreat he sent this telegram. 'I have lost this battle because my force was too small. I again repeat that I am not responsible for this. I feel too earnestly tonight, I have seen too many dead and wounded comrades to feel otherwise that the Govt has not sustained this army.' Those words were delivered. But the officer in charge was too shocked to send the last two lines. We only found out about them later. They read 'If I save this army now I tell you plainly that I own no thanks to you or any other persons in Washington - you have done your best to sacrifice this Army.' "

Rodes and McTeague let that sink in. "Just think of it, Sir, accusing the president and Secretary of War of sacrificing an army while he himself was misusing it in the most cowardly way. And that constant pattern of engage, retreat. Why, Sir, Why?"

"And that line about seeing too many dead and wounded, did you know he never even left his headquarters, never saw the battle? How did he see bodies when he wasn't there?"

"Did you know that after the Battle of Mechanicsville, the very place you were wounded as I understand it, he sent another telegram to Stanton, 'We have again whipped secesh badly...Stonewall Jackson is the victim this time. Victory of today complete and against great odds. I almost begin to think we are invincible.' Yet within hours of sending this, he was retreating again!"

Thomas was beginning to feel he was watching a game of raquets. First one voice, then the other.

"And did you know," McTeague asked a third time, "that he sent Fitz John Porter a telegraph, a telegraph because he himself was nowhere near the actual fighting that said, 'Attack if you can.' And then McClellan turned around, and ordered his headquarters packed up for retreat. He had wagons packed, horses saddled and was ready to bolt away while Porter was fighting."

"This is minor compared to that, but did you also know he sent out orders to all commands, ordering that everything not indispensable to the safety or maintenance of the troops but be abandoned and destroyed? He said, 'This sacrifice is for the short season only, it is hoped...' Millions of dollars of tax payer money went up in smoke." Thomas had indeed heard about that. He was told the fire could be seen for miles!

"And did you know, Sir, that when they finally arrived at Harrison's Landing, a place I understand you spent some time..." They certainly know a lot about me, Thomas thought to himself, "... he sent a telegram to the President. I have not yielded an inch of ground unnecessarily but have retired to prevent the superior force of the Enemy from cutting me off - and take a different base of operations."

"And then he put his printing press to work. Oh, yes, did you know he traveled with his own printing press?" A sheet of newsprint came out of the case. "He used it to share these thoughs with his men. 'I have held you back that you might give the death-blow to the rebellion that has distracted our once happy country.' He wrote, 'I shall soon be on the wing to Richmond-which you can be sure I will take.' "

"According to the Rebel paper we received, they took a different view." Rodes pulled out a Richmond newspaper. "Here's how they reported it." He read, 'Confederate Secretary of Navy Stephen Mallory said, 'The Great McClellan the young Napoleon now like a whipped cur lies on the banks of the James River.' "

"You were there, Sir. You know the army reached the outskirts of Richmond, so close they could hear the bells ring..."

"Yes," Thomas murmured. He did know the army had been that close. He also had to admit their arguments made sense. Some of this he had known; some he had heard, some information had been bits of rumor.

"And then the general put the army in a retreat. His famous change of operations, change of base. He retreated and had the audacity to call it 'the perfect operation, without parallel in the annals of war.' "

"But he even botched the retreat, Sir! We have to ask, why does he do it so poorly? The man is an engineer after all. But after Malvern Hill he used only one muddy road when a total of four roads were available to him. He had a twenty-four hour lead on the rebels, but he made sure the rebels caught up and our forces took heavy losses. Of course one reason the rebels caught up with him is that they used all four of the available roads."

"We also know," McTeague charged, "that in most retreats, the men go first, followed by horses, wagons, etc. But on June 28, McClellan changed the order of retreat. He placed the horses in front, followed by; cattle, wagons and then he placed the men on the road. The soldiers brought up the rear!"

"They marched, Sir, over a single road torn to bits by all those hooves and wheels!"

Both men leaned back and seemed to draw a deep breath in unision.

"So as the senator and the committee see it", Rodes said, "he took a much larger army down to the edges of Richmond and lost his nerve. He lost Union lives and material because he was too timid to fight. Instead of fighting, he took his superior forces and ran, time after time, all the while blaming almost everyone else in the world for his losses. He allowed the rebel army to escape and continue this damned rebellion. It was within his grasp to end the war, but he chose not to! "

"But now, Sir," said Teague, "we move to the more damning items." That comment shocked Thomas. He thought they'd laid out some pretty damaging items already.

"We know that McClellan received plenty of advice telling him that retreating was not only unnecessary but in fact cowardice. General Kearny," as he spoke that name he nodded to Thomas, "Kearny protested. Did you know that?"

"Yes," Thomas said, "he told me some of that."

"According to those present his words were very close to something like this." He pulled another document from the stack. " 'I, Philip Kearny, an old soldier, enter my solemn protest against this order to retreat. We should be launching an attack at Richmond. I say to you all, such as order can only be prompted by cowardice or treason.' "

Rodes jumped in, "General Darius Coach said the retreat took the spirit from the Army of the Potomac. He wrote, 'The soldiers who had fought so magnificently, all last week, marching by night and fighting by day, were now a mob.' They still don't have that spirit today. McClellan stole it from them on the Peninsula."

"Kearny also told McClellan he was being duped. Kearny didn't know it at the time, but our informants now tell us McClellan had 76,000 men at Oak Grove. 76,000 Federals troops! He was held in place by 28,900 Confederates. The evidence shows that Phil Kearny implored Heintzelman to attack again at Oak Grove. 'I know Magruder' he said. "He's a faker, an actor. Let me call his hand!' "

"We also know that Kearny told McClellan that Richmond was lightly defended. He advocated a direct attack. According to those at the meeting, Kearny said. 'The enemy lines around Richmond are thin. They can and must be broken. An order to retreat is wrong! Wrong sir! I ask permission to attack Magruder at once.' "

"General McClellen slammed Kearny down. 'Denied. Nothing has changed, General, the retreat will be made on schedule.' "

"Kearny then erupted! An officer present told us he was sure Kearny was going to be courtmartialed for his outburst. He said the general 'carried on like a madman ... he cried out that it was criminal for a triumphant army to leave the field to a flying foe. His language grew so intemperate that I tried to calm him, but he would not listen. Never had I seen any man that angry.' "

"Then Kearney sent this to his wife, 'With Pope's army I would breathe again. McClellan is the failure I ever proclaimed him. He will only get us into more follies – more waste of blood – fighting by driblets. He has lost the confidence of all...' " He stopped reading and placed the letter on the table. "Kearny was eager for action. He knew that's what the situation called for! That's why he asked to be assigned to Pope!"

The two men quieted to let that sink in. Then, McTeague nodded at Rodes to continue.

"And perhaps most damning, most damning indeed is the fact that twice when he felt battle was imminent, General McClellan deserted his army. He rode away, naming no replacement to command the field in his absence. He sat on the gunboat _Galena_ in the middle of the James River as the Battle of Glendale unfolded. He left no one in charge, nor did he tell people he was leaving. A perfect recipe for disaster, wouldn't you say? Though we can't prove this, several commanders in our army think that if it hadn't have been for some missteps by Lee and

Jackson, the Rebels would have captured and destroyed the Army of the Potomac that day. It certainly looks like McClellan was giving them every chance."

"And lastly, Sir, let us end with this comment. After retreating to Harrison's Landing General McClellan wrote 'I think I begin to see God's wise purpose in all this. If I had succeeded in taking Richmond now, all the fanatics of the North might have been too powerful and reunion impossible.' "

The two men let those words sink in as well. Then they concluded their indictment. "We believe, Sir, General McClellan did not want to win the Peninsula Campaign. Union men died because he did not want to do his duty! He needs to be exposed, Sir. The country needs to know he is a traitor!"

Both men leaned back and placed their crossed hands on their suit vests. "Now we know we've given you a lot to think about..."

"But we are confident of our facts."

"What we propose, Sir, is that you consider our facts and consider a course of action. The committee believes it every man's duty to do his best to put down this rebellion."

"And we hope we can count on you!'"

"Now, may we answer any questions?"

Thomas did not think it was prudent to ask too much, nor did he think they would answer the questions buzzing around his head. Instead he said, "Gentlemen you have made a compelling case. I have to admit I had come to a similiar place myself, but with much less evidence."

Thomas waved at the case and papers on the table. "Impressive. You've given me much to think about. May I have some time?"

"Of course, Sir, of course" said Mr. McTeague.

"But not *too much* time." stressed Mr. Rodes, a slight edge in his voice. "The clock is ticking. The committee most firmly believes this man must be dealt with, and sooner, rather than later."

"Much sooner," said McTeague, "before he can do any more damage to our republic or spill any more precious Union blood!"

Chapter 13

Thomas and Jacob were in their Dodge House rooms sitting at their table. Thomas had notes and papers spread all over the table's surface. Pen and ink stood at the ready. He had made his decision; his next article would be directed, most directed, at General McClellan and his ineptitude.

Thomas had rolled up his sleeves and was ready to go to work. Jacob was helping by organizing Thomas' notes. Mr. Comstock was pushing for another article-fast.

A firm knock on the door interrupted their efforts. They both looked up at the sound. They gave each other a quick 'expecting anyone?' look. Thomas shook his head 'no' as he pushed up from the table.

A bit annoyed at being interrupted, he pulled the door open with a curt, "Yes?"

Then Thomas stumbled back from the door. He was staring wide-eyed, incredulously, at President Abraham Lincoln. The president's frame filled the doorway. Thomas was not a short man, he stood a full six feet, but Mr. Lincoln was a good three if not four inches taller! And that did not count, of course, the famous hat.

The hat was swept off and Mr. Lincoln gave a small bow. "Good evening, Mr. Henderson. I'm sorry to intrude, but might I come in and chat a bit?" As the president moved, Thomas could see a second figure in the hall. A man Thomas knew to be Ward Hill Lamon stood silently behind the president. His reputation as Lincoln's bodyguard was well known. Though Lamon wore a topcoat, Thomas could see the man's revolver. From what he'd heard, Thomas sincerely doubted that was the only weapon Mr. Lamon was carrying.

"Mister…Mister…Mister President!" Thomas managed to stammer. Jacob was frozen in his seat. Thomas somehow managed to return the president's bow and wave him into the room. Jacob, meanwhile, had not moved the first muscle.

"Thank you," said Lincoln as he stepped over the threshold. He paused for a minute to look around. "Very pleasant accommodations." he complimented. Then he turned his attention to Jacob. He stunned Jacob by extending his hand to the boy. "And you are…?"

"Jacob Bunten, Sir." he answered in a strangled whisper. But then he recovered enough to add in a slightly stronger voice, "From Indiana!"

The president gave a small laugh. "Might that be from Salem, Indiana, Mr. Bunten?" His eyes twinkled. "Fine town. One of my secretaries was born there. And you may know I spent some time in the Great State of Indiana myself."

"Oh, yes, Sir," Jacob quickly answered. "I know all about your time in Indiana!"

"All about it, hey?" Mr. Lincoln laughed again. He shook his head. "Well, I wonder if I should worry that you know all about me. I'm sure there were some shenanigans I don't want remembered." He paused and then gave

Jacob a sly look, "Know about the footprints on the ceiling?"

"Oh, no, Sir," Jacob began but Lincoln smiled and raised a hand to assure the boy that all was well.

He turned to Thomas, who sat with a stunned look on his face. "How in the world could Mr. Lincoln know where Jacob was from?" he was asking himself.

"May I sit?" the president asked.

Thomas, embarrassed he had not offered the president a chair, said immediately, "Of course, Sir. Anywhere."

Mr. Lincoln took the few short steps to the table, tucking his long legs as he sat. "Gentlemen, I shall come right to it. I have intruded on your pleasant evening because I have a favor to ask."

"Anything!" Thomas instantly replied. "Anything!'

Jacob said nothing. He simply could believe he was sitting with the president of the United States.

Mr. Lincoln smiled again. "Thomas, if I may call you that, I've read your stories with interest. You're becoming a fine writer."

That comment stunned Thomas. The president had read his work?

"And recently, your articles have made quite a splash." The president reached into his inner pocket and pulled out a folded New York *Constitutionalist*. The paper was folded open to Thomas' last article. The president gently laid the newspaper on the table.

Thomas felt an odd twinge of…unease? Had he done something wrong? Was he in trouble with the president?

Mr. Lincoln then gently dropped his large hand down on the folded *Constitutionalist*. "But I would have to conclude from having read your last article, that you no longer hold our current commanding general in very high regard.

And there it was. The reason for the visit. Thomas looked at Lincoln, expectantly.

"Now let me quickly say Thomas, that I find argument with very few of your facts."

This certainly surprised Thomas. He had jumped to the conclusion that he was in trouble with the president.

"And let me say, I am a great supporter of the freedom of the press and the First Amendment."

Those words chilled Thomas a bit. On the surface they were supportive, but Thomas also had heard about last summer's raids on newspapers and newspaper editors. He knew over two hundred papers had been menaced. He also knew some newspaper editors had been imprisoned. So he wondered, was he being threatened? His thoughts jumped to the silent armed man standing outside his door.

"No," Lincoln continued, "I support the press. Why, did you know I even owned a newspaper? Well, part of one. Back in Springfield, a small thing but still a going concern." Mr. Lincoln rubbed the bridge of his nose with two long fingers. "But that does not mean I applaud everything everyone writes. Some of the things that appear in print never should have been written."

"But not your article, Thomas. No, I have no quarrels with it. That's not why I am here." He gazed directly at Thomas. "I do not argue with the facts you laid out. However, I did come to ask you not to write any more articles on General McClellan-at least for the time being."

Thomas was very confused. His article was accurate yet he was being asked to be silent about General McClellan?

"To cut to the chase, Thomas, it is simply that I need McClellan. I need him now." Mr. Lincoln raised a hand, forestalling any comments. "I realize he is flawed. I realize he has made a great many mistakes. But he is the commanding general, he is on hand now, right this minute. And frankly, I need a commanding general right this minute. Lee is on the move, for that matter the whole rebel army is on the move. They have a commanding general. I, in turn, must have a commanding general. And McClellan is currently that man." The president paused and looked at Thomas for his reaction.

Thomas truly did not know how to respond. He sat silently for a minute, deciding how much to say. Finally he took the plunge. "But, but Mr. Lincoln, he's not fit! He's not a fighter. He can't stay!" He pointed at the *Constitutionalist* on the table. "You know the mistakes he's made. Sir, he is costing us the war!" Thomas suddenly stopped, aware that he might indeed have just gone too far.

But surprisingly, Mr. Lincoln just leaned back, stretching his arms above his head. "Yes, yes, all true. But it is also true that I need him now, today. Let me see if I can make this clearer." The president leaned a bit farther back in the chair. It creaked. He then leaned forward directing the full presidential gaze on Thomas and Jacob.

"Now you see, I do understand the power of the press. I've said it before and I believe it, public sentiment is crucial." He gently patted the folded newspaper. "And nothing shapes public sentiments today more quickly that our newspapers."

Thomas and Jacob sat silently, taking in the president's words.

"I grant you we have a conundrum." the president continued. "I say your article is factual and then I ask you to not write another factual article on this subject. It's a head-scratcher for sure." He gave his two companions a sad smile. "But if we have more articles like this, then the public may well be swayed away from General McClellan. If all lose faith in him, and I have no one better ready to move into the position, we may well lose the war. So as I weigh things," he moved his hands in an up and down balancing motion, "it seems to come down to keeping the nation's confidence about the general on the one hand, and having one more article out there on the other. Do you see what I mean?" The hands continued to see saw back and forth.

Jacob sat staring at the president, nodding his head in agreement. It made perfect sense to him. Of course the country needed a leader. The army needed a commander.

The president looked at Jacob, smiled and nodded back at him.

"It's like I told Senator Wade…" he paused and gave Thomas a cryptic look, "you may have spoken with him, perhaps…" and another chill passed through Thomas as he received the message. "The senator kindly paid a call on me, letting me know I should sack General McClellan. 'And replace him with whom?' I asked the good senator. He said, 'Why with anyone!' I let him know anyone was fine for him, but I needed someone."

"Thomas, I have come to understand a great many things over the last few months." The president took another sad pause. "Yes, a great many things indeed. I know without doubt it is a challenge to be the general of a huge army. It is an almost impossible task to put down a rebellion. I'm sure very few of us could do it."

Thomas nodded his agreement to this sentiment. It was certainly not a job he would like. Anyone can issue commands and draw lines on a map but making sense of a battle and leading a nation to victory? That was a different story altogether.

"And to have any hope of victory, you must have the country behind you, that popular sentiment I mentioned. Well," he said giving the two a small smile, "at least it's good to have 51% of that popular sentiment."

Suddenly Mr. Lincoln pushed away from the table and started stretching his arms and upper body. "Hmmmmph! Can't sit as long as I used to," he apologized. "need to move." He completed a few gyrations and then turned back to Thomas. "So you see, Sir, to sum up my point, I need a commanding general."

Thomas nodded. He understood the president's point so far.

The president then turned to Jacob. "And what about you, Jacob? Do you take my point?"

After a split second of frozen silence, Jacob gushed, "Oh my goodness, yes, Mr. President!"

Thomas and the president laughed. "Fine, I just wanted to make sure."

Thomas did understand the president's points, but they did not answer all his questions. He took a deep breath considering. Then he said, "I believe I do understand your point, Sir,…"

"But?" Mr. Lincoln interjected.

"Yes sir, but may I ask…what about the facts in the articles? Don't we agree the facts were correct?' Thomas thought a bit more and then plunged on. "Well, straight out, Sir, isn't General McClellan a bad general? Shouldn't the public know? Doesn't the country deserve to know?"

The president reached out and patted Thomas' arm with a surprisingly gentle touch. "They most certainly do. And we have an obligation to make sure they know all the facts. They need the whole story, but here's the rub, Thomas, we haven't provide that to them yet."

"Now your article is a step, a big step. It provides the people with many facts." The president stopped and looked directly into Thomas' eyes. "But we've not provided them with all the facts. It's our job to provide them the whole story when we can."

Thomas pushed back a bit. "But, Sir, how can we provide the story by withholding the facts?"

Now Lincoln the attorney answered. "Not by withholding facts, but releasing them so they tell the whole story." He paused a minute, idly rubbing his arms together across his chest. "And you could not have done that you see. You, Thomas, don't have all the facts. You don't have the whole story."

The president settled back in his chair. "Yes, General McClellan has made mistakes, huge ones, but he's not the only one who has. You need to know that I've made mistakes too, equally big ones. And those mistakes hampered General McClellan efforts."

"After Bull Run…" he shook his head again. "Such a black time!" he said in a deeply sad voice. He was staring at the table but he wasn't seeing it. He was back in Manassas, Virginia, reliving the horror. Then his gaze left the table and he looked at Thomas. "I understand you were there?"

Once again, Thomas was caught completely off guard. How much did this man know about them? Instead of speaking, Thomas simply nodded.

"Now you see, there is an example of one of my bad mistakes. I pushed General McDowell to move before the army was ready. I was so sure we could end the rebellion with that great push, one push, one battle, one day. I was sure it would be over."

Thomas nodded in agreement. After all, he'd believed those things, too.

"But sadly I was wrong. I wronged those boys and I wronged their general." He paused again. "Thomas, everyday of my life I'm aware that I have blood from that battle on my hands." Unconsciously, the president rubbed his hands together. "But after that battle, after I saw those green untrained men come running back to Washington, I changed horses. I wanted a new general, a general who could whip those boys into an army, I found that general in General McClellan."

"Now whatever you think of him today, I believe in my bones that General McClellan was the man to reform, refit and retrain those men into what became the Army of the Potomac. He seemed to have it all; youth energy, intelligence, training. Why if memory serves, I believe you also came to appreciate many of those same abilities."

"True enough," Thomas thought, "The things I saw him do, he did very well. I just did not know then that he could not fight."

The president was moving on. "Perhaps if I had given General McDowell the same chance I gave General McClellan the results would have been different." he mused, "But I didn't so that was that."

"So as I look at it now, I needed three things then - I immediately needed a new commander; fair or not, the nation wasn't standing for McDowell, and remember we were a fragile nation, as I believe we are now. I needed a leader who could come in and command respect. McClellan did that. After all, he'd already won victories. I also needed a person who could whip a mob into shape. McClellan did all that. Now, at the same time, I also needed a general who could lead that new army to victory." He paused and gave a very sad smile to Thomas. "And you've so accurately pointed out, McClellan can't do that. But I did not know that at the time, so that fault is mine. He did however proceed to do the first three things I asked."

"I made another major mistake. I saw but failed to realize General McClellan and I were of different worlds. We had different goals. You see, we spoke a common language to a point. We both wanted to preserve the Union, but I've come to believe that while we used the same phrase, we meant very different things."

"We were both Whigs in the tradition of Henry Clay and Daniel Webster. I believed we shared their commitment to the preservation of the Union. But after his Harrison's Landing letter..." the president paused to give Thomas a questioning look. Thomas nodded his understanding. The president continued. "I came to see that when he says he wants the Union reunited, he means to go back to the status quo-including slavery."

Lincoln stared into space. Then he said, "And frankly, Thomas, that is just no longer possible. Now to be fair, I think I may have started at the same place as the good general, though I believe I have been against slavery for years. However, I did say that if I could preserve the Union and preserve slavery, I would do so."

"But you also said a house divided against itself cannot stand!" Both Lincoln and Henderson were startled by Jacob's comment and laughed.

"True enough, Mr. Bunten, true enough. And the more we've gotten the tail on the horse, the more I've come to believe that is indeed true. Certainly after the bloodshed at the Battle of Shiloh, I began to see that even more clearly."

"But returning to the point, I do readily acknowledge that McClellan has a gifted, perhaps even brilliant military talent for organizing and training. The man, after all, is an engineer. I honestly do believe that if he could have carried out his plan exactly as it was drawn up, it would have worked. But the plan did not go exactly as drawn and maybe part of that is my fault. When Stonewall Jackson attacked, we panicked. Maybe I panicked. We did not think the capital was safe. Looking at it now, I can clearly see that was not the case. Jackson was a small force fifty miles away. Did I take troops away that McClellan could have used? Had I sent him McDowell, would he have taken Richmond? I know now that while Stonewall Jackson retreated south, more than 60,000 Union troops sat idle in the Valley without an enemy to fight."

"But, Sir," Thomas responded, "it wouldn't have mattered! McClellan didn't use the troops he had. Look how he misused General Kearney. More troops wouldn't have mattered."

Lincoln nodded. "You may well be right, Thomas. But he was right that I was being fooled. Even General McDowell wrote, 'I shall gain nothing for you there and shall lose much for you here...it throws us all back and from Richmond north we shall have large masses paralyzed.'" Mr. Lincoln shook his head sadly. "General

McClellan pleaded with me to release those troops." He leaned back and closed his eyes. "Basically, as I remember it he said something like… 'I beg you to reconsider the order…the success of our case will be imperiled by so greatly reducing my force when it is actually under the fire of the enemy.' "

"I waved him off, Thomas. I replied 'You now have over 100,000 troops with you. I think you better break the enemy's line from Yorktown to Warwick River at once.' And of course that did not happen."

"But honestly, Thomas, we could almost put all of that aside because of one single crucial fact." The president turned to Jacob. "Did you know, Jacob, that you and I shared some time in Virginia?"

Jacob nodded his head quickly. "Yes, Sir, I did! In fact, I saw you! I was there when you were ordering the taking of the port of Norfolk and the sinking of the *Virginia*! Mr. Henderson was elsewhere, but I saw you!" He was very pleased with himself.

"Well, I'm sorry I did not see you, Jacob. And to be fair, the army had more to do with the taking of Norfolk and the rebels had more to do with the sinking of the *Virginia*. But yes, I was there. And I actually returned a second time when I went to Harrison's Landing. And of all the things I learned on those trips, one fact emerged time after time. One fact trumped all others. And that fact, gentlemen, was the Army of the Potomac."

"Sir?" Thomas asked.

"The soldiers, Thomas, the soldiers. Everywhere I went, I heard the soldiers talk. Some men believed what

General McClellan was telling them. Some didn't. But very few of them blamed the general. Some blamed Congress. Some blamed the rebs, some blamed my cabinet and some blamed me. But virtually no man I talked to, and I shook a great many hands, blamed General McClellan. They still believed in him."

Lincoln now turned his full gaze on Thomas. "And that is what we must have. Belief. If the men in the army believe we will fail, we lose this war tomorrow. If they believe in McClellan, no matter how many change of bases they endure, they will fight. And that is what we must have - a fighting army. But if McClellan is pulled away, if he is sacked, how will that army respond? Will they stay if they believe he was misused? If the army leaves me now, well, that firing will have done me no good. The rebels take the battlefield, they take the city, they take the war. And Thomas, I believe our men believe in General McClellan this very day. Do you see what I mean?"

Thomas was struck by the president's argument. It was suddenly easy to see how true it was. He had never thought about it that way, but now he realized the president was one hundred percent correct. McClellan was an outright failure as a fighting general but he had created an army that could fight. And that army still marched with McClellan. Lincoln and the country had to have that army, so for today at least, Lincoln and the nation needed McClellan.

Then a new thought troubled Thomas. "But Sir, what about the committee?"

Lincoln gave a rueful smile. "Well, it won't be easy, but I think I can handle them. I have virtually no military experience, well, except for the Black Hawk War and that proved how little I really knew, but those men have even less knowledge and military experience. I do have some experience, experience with devices, technology. Those men think we are fighting wars like they did in the past. But I understand that we've moved past the age of Napoleon. No, that's not true, I've been taught we've moved past the age of Napoleon. I understand how guns have changed for instance. I know the new rifled muskets have increased accuracy since the days of George Washington. I believe the committee members do not appreciate the new world of war."

"I don't believe those men have an idea of what it takes to move an army. They look at a map, draw a line on it and blithely say 'Move your army there!' But it does not work that way-moving an army. I've come to learn that it is almost an impossible undertaking. The men on the committee do not understand that. They do not understand the true nature of war today. They are blind to it."

"You are correct in believing they dislike McClellan. They dislike him because he did not win, because he was slow and they dislike him because he is a Democrat. I believe I can fix everything-except him being a Democrat. And does bring me to one last thought."

He paused for the smallest minute before continuing. "Now, Thomas, I would never order you or coerce you but if you choose to agree with me on this I could help..."

"Oh, no, Mr. Lincoln, I couldn't...!" Thomas immediately protested, making an assumption.

The president smiled. "I really wasn't trying to bribe you, Thomas, though I can see why you might think so."

Thomas turned bright red with embarrassment. He had just accused the president of the United States of bribery!

"No, I was going to point out that if you choose to agree with me on this, and stayed at the Constitutionalist, there could be problems for you. I don't think the committee will think kindly of you if you return to writing and no more anti-McClellan articles appear. They may be blind to the war situation, but they still have great power. I think you would be in more than a spot of trouble and I would feel responsible. Should you no longer be a journalist however, I can see no problem."

Thomas really did not know where the president was going with this. Was he losing his job?

But the president was heading in a different direction. "I have need of a new White House assistant, and Thomas, I am offering the job to you."

The president continued. "Might you have heard of Lawrence Gobright? He's the New York Associated Press Washington Bureau chief. I've had some workings with the man. I need a man to liaison with him and to do other special assignments that I may deem necessary." Mr. Lincoln turned and looked at Jacob. "And it could very well turn out that my new assistant might need an assistant." With this the president suddenly pushed away from the table and rose. "The job offer is a real one. I will await your response."

"But the job offer is almost a side issue. The most important thing to decide is what you think about my arguments. Of course you must make up your own mind and I will respect your decision. You may find my arguments weak. You may decide to continue your current course of action and stay at the *Constitutionalist*. You may decide to write articles damning General McClellan. Certainly all these action would be within your rights.

But as I said, I felt compelled to offer my version of the facts, the facts as I see them. Now you can make your best decision. So I ask, please give it some thought and please consider my job offer. It is indeed a serious job offer. As I said, you're becoming a fine writer and you have talents I can certainly use."

"And with that" the president said, firmly planting the famous hat on his head, "I will leave you. I have taken enough of your evening. I hope to hear from you soon. Gentlemen, it was a pleasure to meet you both. I bid you goodnight."

Another bow and as quickly as he had come, the president was gone.

Chapter 14

For a second the only sound in the Dodge House room was the solid click of the closing door. Then Thomas and Jacob began excitedly chattering, each talking over the other.

"Can you believe that?"

"Did it really happen?"

"I shook the hand of the president!"

"He knew my hometown!"

"He'd read my articles!!"

They were going so hard, they were using all the oxygen in the room.

The two finally settled down and began to discuss the president's visit. As Thomas evaluated both sides of the argument, he realized he was sincerely torn. He deeply believed McClellan was the wrong man to be commanding the Army of the Potomac. He deeply believed that McClellan had harmed the country and probably had extended the war. At the same time, he did indeed understand the president's point. The commanding general was of course important, but in the end, clearly he was not as important as the men. "We must keep the loyalty of the men. They are all!" he concluded.

Thomas was also torn because agreeing with Mr. Lincoln would mean leaving journalism. He understood that Senator Wade, for one, would be very unhappy with him if anything but anti-McClellan articles appeared under his byline. He would not care to enjoy another visit from Misters McTeague and Rodes. He had enjoyed writing and enjoyed journalism. He believed, without too much conceit, that he had become a semi-decent reporter. It would be hard to leave that. But if he left journalism, Wade couldn't really say too much on the matter.

And to be leaving for the White House? A job in the White House? He didn't really care if he were the assistant to the assistant of the assistant, to be working in the White House. Oh, my! And who was to say, that after the war, he couldn't return to journalism, if he was so drawn? What might he bring to a job with White House experience?

Jacob, on the other hand, was not torn at all. Mr. Lincoln's words were all he needed to hear. And he was thrilled to his Indiana boots to be going to the White House. Never in his wildest dreams had he imagined anything like this!

In the end Thomas came to the same conclusion. Not just because the president had spoken to him but because upon serious reflection, he had come to believe that the president was right. Thomas knew how fragile a country could be. He had seen the Union dissolve and seen Virginia, the state that everyone said could never leave, leave. He had come to the conclusion that General George B. McClellan was gifted as an organizer but incredibly incompetent as a fighting general. But he also had to agree with Mr. Lincoln's logic. Right now, right now at least, Little Napoleon was best choice.

And perhaps most importantly, Thomas knew the men loved Little Mac and he knew the importance of that love. If Mr. Lincoln did not have another man ready to step in, a man who could produce more results than McClellan had, well it was just not the time to make such a change. Thomas came to his decision. He would resign from the *Constitutionalist*. He realized he was at peace with the decision. Thomas knew the president fully understood the general's shortcomings and that he was actively looking for a replacement. Until that time, until Mac was gone, Thomas would hold his tongue. He still knew what he knew; he knew General Kearny was right. He knew he had a story the American people deserved to read. But for now he would leave journalism and leave that story for another day.

That did leave one rather large issue on the table, however. Once he resigned, of course, he still had to pay the rent, so...

One week later, Thomas, and Jacob both found themselves at the White House, ready to learn about their new jobs. They had presented themselves at the front door and were astonished to be ushered into the president's presence. He was talking with a man neither Thomas nor Jacob recognized. "Gentlemen" Mr. Lincoln called out. "Welcome to the White House. We are so pleased to have you here." He shook hands with both Thomas and Jacob. Then he turned toward the other man. "Allow me to introduce Mr. John Hay, one of my secretaries. You may be interested to know, Jacob, Mr. Hay is also from Salem, Indiana.

"Yes, indeed," Hay answered, "born right downtown in Salem on South College Street!" He shook hands with each, "Pleasure to meet you both!" Jacob stood stunned. College Street was but a street over from his Pa's store. This man was from Salem?

Mr. Lincoln walked over and opened a door. "Nicolay?" he called. A second man walked into the room. "And this is the other scoundrel that seems to get me in so much trouble, Mr. John Nicolay. Nicolay is John Hay's partner in all this, my other secretary. You'll have to forgive him, Jacob, he's not from Indiana. Believe it or not, Jacob," Mr. Lincoln said in a low tone, "he attended school in Cincinnati."

Jacob thought, "Cincinnati? Why's that just a skip, jump and a throw from home! Both of these men..."

He was interrupted by a knock on the doorframe. A third man entered the room. His face was buried in a stack of papers and he spoke as he walked into the room. "Mr. Lincoln, I've read this as you asked, and I believe..." He stopped as he looked up to see the occupants of the room. He came to an abrupt halt. "Oh, forgive me Mr. President, I thought you and Mr. Hay were alone. I certainly did not mean to intrude. I apologize." He was waving his hands and the stack of papers by way of an apology and had become red faced.

"No, no, no, Mr. Dana, please come in. There are people here I want you to meet. Thomas Henderson, Jacob Bunten, meet Charles Dana." Mr. Lincoln continued, "Mr.

Dana here is an employee of the war department. His title is Special Investigating Agent, but I call him my eyes of the administration. Mr. Dana, Mr. Henderson and Mr. Bunten. Newest members of this administration." said Mr Lincoln pointing at each in turn. They shook hands. "Mr. Dana, if you will but wait a moment?" He turned to John Nicolay.

"Now Nicolay, would you please take our two new employees and get them acquainted with their jobs? Give them a taste of what life around here is like!"

And with that, Thomas and Jacob left journalism and started new lives. Neither could believe where their journey had taken them. Interestingly, they both had similar thoughts. "The White House!! Now where is this taking me? What's next?"

Made in the USA
Middletown, DE
31 May 2023